FOUR ROOMS

J. A. WYNTERS

Four Rooms

Editing by: Spell bound editing

Cover design: The Dust Jacket Designs

Interior Formatting: Dawn Lucous, Yours Truly Book Services

Dean

The casino is busy, as always. A room full of addicts all pulled by invisible cerebral hooks made of false hope and blaring lights. Inside these walls, we are all high on neurochemicals while our pockets are slowly being drained. But I'm not here for the games. I'm here for the hunt, but if that fails, there's always the booze. Sure, it's more expensive than my local bar and tastes just the same, but there is something about the lights that never go out, the ringing machines in the background and the throbbing of people around me, that makes me feel like I could actually belong.

This is my third whiskey, and the burn feels just as fresh as the first and just as satisfying. There's an old lady who's been sitting on one machine for the last hour. Her only movements, the pulling of the crank and the occasional shift in her chair. Her lips are chapped, and her eyes glossed over. It's a look most people get when they spend enough time here.

Most nights are the same; fools and losers all dressed up

trying to fill up on hope, seduced by empty promises. But tonight, I spot *her*.

She walks into the casino and heads straight for the bar. I notice her because of the dress she wears—she seems overdressed—even for a place such as this where you see all kinds. It's a long cerulean dress held up by a single thin strap across one shoulder. It hugs her stunning figure, pushing up her full breasts and twirling down into shocks of midnight blue, with whispers of silver hiding among the indigo fabric. Her long locks of blonde hair curl down her naked back and her lips are a shade of fuck-me red that glistens under the bar lights. It looks as though she's stepped out of a fashion magazine and stumbled into this place.

She orders a drink and takes a card out of her little clutch, giving the barman a crooked smile as he looks her up and down and up again, taking a few extra seconds to stare at her nipples which push through the fabric. He hands her a cocktail; something pink and no doubt sweet, and she scans the room taking everything in slowly. Rows upon rows of machines, tables set out in the middle; poker, blackjack, baccarat and everything in between. Her gaze lingers on one of the tables, a high roller game with a few hotshot wannabes. Three men sit at the table and one seat remains open. She drains her drink then orders another. When she turns back to the room, our eyes meet, and I tip my drink towards her giving her one of my better smiles. She returns the gesture with one of her own, and I decide it's time to introduce myself. This night finally has potential.

Sliding off my chair, I take a step towards her, our eyes still locked, when a sweet-looking brunette cuts off my path and gives me a glowing smile. "There you are."

ROOM #217 A CASE OF MISTAKEN IDENTITY

Dean

"Excuse me?" My gaze leaves the stunner at the bar and sweeps over the newcomer now blocking my way.

"You are him, aren't you?"

"Him?"

"Mark?" She leans in a little and whispers, "From Casual Cupid. It's me Margot."

I have to admit I am perplexed and slightly intrigued. When I look towards the bar, the woman in the blue dress is making her way to the unoccupied seat at the blackjack table, and I inhale my disappointment and irritation as I focus my attention on the woman in front of me. She's slim, wearing a sexy black number that hugs her petite figure, and the way she's anxiously biting her lip makes me wonder what else she could do with that mouth of hers.

When I take too long to answer, red begins to flood her face, spreading across her cheeks and down her neck. "Oh my god, it's not you. I'm so sorry, I just thought..." She starts looking around frantically. "I've been looking for fifteen minutes, and I was so sure it's you..."

There's a part of me that wants her to be mortified, after all, she just fucked up my plans for blue dress, but then there's another part of me, the curious part of me that doesn't want this woman going home thinking she's been stood up, and of course there is that mouth...

"Yes, I'm him. Sorry you've been looking for so long, I just got stuck at the bar. The service here is terrible."

She gives me a shaky smile as relief washes over her face. "You look different than you do in your picture."

"And you look stunning," I say and mostly, I mean it. She smiles at me, and I think I have settled her nerves a little. As I gesture to an empty table, I can't help but wonder who this Mark is and why he has stood her up. I realise as I pull her chair out for her, that I am treading a thin line. I have no idea who this woman is, what this app is and what conversations she and this 'Mark' might have had. On the upside, alcohol tends to blur all those lines, so maybe with a few drinks in her she can go home smiling and maybe not think too badly of that asshole who left her to the likes of me. "Drink?"

"That would be great."

It would be great. It would also be my fourth in the last hour and I should possibly slow down; then again, I won't be getting the kind of action I want tonight, so no need to keep my wits about me.

"What would you like?"

"You know what I like." She winks at me, and I am at a loss already, though I won't lie, my cock twitches at the fact that her tone implies more than what she's saying.

"Remind me?"

She frowns at me, and I'm already blowing it. "Mai tai of course."

"Of course." I grin at her and make my way to the bar where I order her cocktail and another whiskey for myself.

The barman is taking ages. I glance over at my new friend and smile at her. She eyes me with suspicion, but it fades and her mouth splits in a cheeky smile. I think about another good use for that mouth of hers.

Finally, the barman arrives and hands me our drinks. I turn around to return to our table when someone blocks my way. I move to avoid them just to have half my drinks spill all over my hands. Fuck.

"Shit." When I look up, two stunning brown eyes and a beautiful face stare back at me.

"I'm sorry," says the girl in the blue dress, and suddenly I don't give a fuck about the drinks or the woman waiting for me at the table, whose name I am already forgetting.

"It's fine." And it is. I set the spilt drinks back on the bar. My fingers are sticky, and for a split second I wonder how deep I could shove them into her mouth before she gags as she sucks them clean. I bat the thought away, she doesn't look the type, there's an innocence about her, probably why she's so appealing.

"Oh, I really am so sorry. Let me replace those."

I rub my hands on my jeans to dry them. "No, it's fine, I should have been watching where I was going."

"You should have. Are you sure you don't have a drinking problem?" She makes a point to look at both glasses before tilting her head slightly to one side.

A slow smile creeps across my face. She's feisty too. I can't help but wonder what she'd look like putting up a fight. "You should be careful with that joke, it's an antique."

"You wouldn't know a joke if it bit you on the ass" she counters, and I bite down on my lip keeping my smile at bay.

I lean in closer and get a whiff of her sweet perfume; it's intoxicating and lovely, but I wonder what she smells like underneath it. "If someone was going to bite me on the ass, she had better have bought me dinner first."

Her mouth falls open in a gasp making a perfect little O, and my inside's clench. She draws a breath and seems like she's about to come back with a retort, but the fucking barman chooses that moment to place our drinks down and ask for his money. I hand him my credit card without taking my eyes off her face.

"I said I'd get the drinks." She pouts.

"And I said it was fine." The barman returns, and I'm forced to look away from her to retrieve my card.

"Thank you," she says as she reaches for her pink cocktail. "It was nice to meet you...?"

"Dean." I give her one of my sweetest smiles even as she is dismissing me, somehow this doesn't feel like a complete loss.

"It was nice to meet you, Dean, I'm Isi."

Isi. "Have a great night, Isi." I tip my drink towards her and make my way back to the woman in the black dress who sits in wait at our table.

"Slow service." She looks at me for a second and her eyes drift towards Isi. I can't say that I blame her, that kind of beauty has gotten cities burned to the ground. "But it comes with a smile." I give her my best one, goofy and charming all at once, and as predicted, she smiles back and some of the tension melts away from around her eyes. I set the drinks down, and she takes a long sip out of hers. I chuckle. "Do I make you nervous?"

"Not at all, I guess it's just been a while since I've been out on a date, let alone a blind date."

I cock an eyebrow and nod, my fingers playing with the condensation on my glass. "That's okay, most of the basics are the same, but a few things have changed."

"Such as?" She looks at me over her mai tai.

"For one, women pay for dinner now, and secondly, sex is guaranteed."

"What?" She pulls an overly shocked face and an over-the-top gasp. "Well let me tell you what's guaranteed, I'm *not* paying for dinner." She winks at me, and I can't help the smirk that spreads across my lips.

"Damn, I was hoping for a free meal." I watch her cheeks change to a lovely shade of pink.

She takes another long sip before she starts, "So tell me about yourself."

"Why? That's boring first date stuff. Let's do something different." I divert, unsure what she and Mark might have exchanged in their app conversations.

"Such as?" She leans in and focuses her attention on my face.

"Tell me two things you suck at."

She leans back into her chair and frowns a little. "Mm." Her fingers shoot out and start playing on the rim of her glass. I guess I do make her nervous. "Well, I am a very aggressive driver—I mean, other people just don't know how to drive."

"Obviously." I chuckle a little picturing this tiny woman screaming profanities and using a lead foot to plough through traffic. It's an amusing image.

"And I can't iron. Or draw a straight line... even with a ruler. It's like a talent but a terrible and useless one to have." She shakes her head at that last one. It's sweet the way she mocks herself.

"If it makes you feel any better, I can just about draw a stick figure... *just*. And how aggressive are we talking here?"

"I don't know you well enough to share those details with you yet."

I can't help but laugh at her. She's cute. She has potential. "Fair play, but just FYI, ironing is one of my favourite things to do."

She scoffs at me. "I hate it and I'm no good at it."

"Well, I'll be happy to do yours for a price."

"Oh? Name your price." She crosses her hands over her chest. Things just got a little more interesting.

I drag my thumb over my lower lip as I think and watch her eyes following my movements as she bites her own. A slow smile spreads across my face, and I know she won't be paying for dinner cause after this drink we will move on to the next part of the night. "The price will depend on how much I have to do."

"Not much, I only have two button-up shirts."

I pout. "Oh. Then there might not be much in it for me after all."

She shrugs and takes a slow sip of her drink.

"I take it back. On second thought, it sounds quite lucrative."

"I don't know, might be too late." She leans closer over the table and her eyes crash with mine. "But if it's important to you, I'll give you one more opportunity to name your best price."

"Both shirts for a drink sounds completely fair to me. Of course, you can tip as you please." I wink at her, and her eyes flash as she looks at my lips.

"A tip, hey?"

"It's standard practice."

"I see." She licks her lips, and I can't help but notice how red her lipstick is and how it would look so beautiful smeared all over her fucking face. "Will you travel to pick up said shirts or..." she breaks through my thoughts.

"I guess I can do that... Anything else you'll need me to do whilst I stop by?"

"Can you fix a dishwasher?"

"I'd give it a go. What kind of tip would that give me?"

"That depends on how good your plumbing is. I can't make promises about a tip until I receive the service."

"I'll consider it a hefty tip then." I hold up my hands and wiggle them in front of her. "These magic fingers can work wonders."

"Time will tell." She acts nonchalant, and suddenly my fingers want to shove themselves up her pussy and show her exactly the kind of workmanship I am capable of. "You'll be judged for your work, so it best not be shoddy."

"There'll be no shoddiness found."

"I don't know, I've been let down by plumbers before."

"You deserve better."

"I think so too." She winks at me and drains the remainder of her drink.

"So... how do you propose we test out my workmanship?"

"Well..." She bites her lower lip, sucking it into her mouth, and her cheeks turn a shade of dark pink. "I've booked a room..."

"Presumptuous." I fold my arms across my chest and cock my head to the left.

"Hopeful." She winks at me.

"Well, I'll be more than happy to give the pipes a good service, but not sure they have a dishwasher upstairs."

"We won't know till we go look now, will we?" She stands and puts her bag over her shoulder looking at me. I stay seated for another beat, not because I don't intend to go upstairs with her but because it gives me a sick little pleasure watching her sure face fall slightly at my hesitation. I like these two sides of her. One commanding, flirtatious and confident, one flailing and in need of a helping hand to lead her down a path she recognises, to a place she can be confident again. I like that I am that hand for her now. And as I stand, she schools her face, and that flirtatious wildcat comes out again. She is going to be fun. Not the fun I was hoping for with Isi, but fun, nonetheless.

I take one last lingering look at Isi as we make our way to the elevator. It pings and I let Margot take the lead as she presses the floor button and leans provocatively against the back wall. Sure, she is sexy as hell, but she's not the kind of girl I usually take home.

The elevator stops and we walk out. She takes the lead, and I follow, watching her ass swing as she walks. She does have a sexy-as-fuck ass, and I know exactly what I'm about to do to it. She did say her dishwasher needed a good service, but maybe she doesn't realise it has a number of ways to get fixed.

She slides the card into its slot and the door opens. She walks inside and leans against the wall, giving me a look. *The* look. The one that says, *well we're here now so you better get your tool belt on.*

I pounce. Because that's what this wildcat wants. An animal.

Grabbing her hands, I pin them over her head and pull up forcing her onto her tiptoes. She sucks in a sharp breath as I do this, and I pull harder, her smaller frame almost dangling, like a marionette with tight strings.

I sink my teeth into her throat and listen to her moan, the sound vibrating through my teeth.

My hand slithers under her dress, and I work my way up. I don't explore her body in the way I usually would, don't take my time. I know what she wants. My hand slides into her underwear, and I find her soaked. Just as I knew she would be. As my fingers roll over her clit, she moans and tries to pull her hands out of my grip and into a more comfortable position, but I pin her down and push two fingers inside her. She gasps at the intrusion. It's a lovely sound that makes my cock harder. Yanking her underwear down, I push them down her legs and they cling to her tanned, smooth thighs.

My fingers slide in and out of her easily, and she tries to grind against me, but the way I have her suspended makes it impossible; if she moves, she will lose her footing. She strains against me, and I smile against her skin. Her hands try to force themselves away. I know she wants to touch me, and the way she keeps looking at me and biting her lips tells me her mouth is searching for mine. But I don't want her to kiss me, not yet. I'd rather her mouth keeps making these sweet little sounds.

I pull my fingers out and draw long slow circles around her clit. She whimpers for me as I do, trying to move, wanting to participate in her own pleasure. I move my fingers away and slide inside her again. She moans, part in pleasure, part in disappointment, and I coat myself with her wetness before pulling out again and circling her clit. She keeps trying to guide me, but I won't allow it. I keep up my little game. This little wildcat has turned into a mouse that can't get away and she is lovely to play with. Each time I circle a little longer, pushing her a little closer to her orgasm, and each time I pull away, she crumples at the disappointment.

"Please," she begs. I love it when they beg. They always do towards the end like somehow it will change the outcome. Like somehow, it will allow them some form of control, like somehow, they can appeal to my better judgement. But she won't.

"Shhhhh, everything will be okay," I assure her as my fingers are back on her clit, and tears begin to pool in her eyes like it's already too much and she wants it to end, but I've only just started.

"Don't stop."

I smile as I do, and her frustration ripples through me. Desperation is a delightful feeling to feed off. My fingers brush over her clit; a few whispered touches that have her shivering. Fuck, she looks so sexy all helpless and vulnerable, hanging in my grip. Maybe this wasn't such a wasted night after all. A sheen of sweat covers her flushed face and her breath is an erratic pattern of desperate pants.

I hold there a few more seconds letting her feel that burn between her legs, the ache in her shoulders, the strain of her feet trying to find the ground, and then I start again, my fingers circling nice and slow, around and around, teasing, holding her at bay at the precipice.

"Please," she begs again, and this time I don't stop. But I also don't speed up, not like I know she wants me to, *needs* me to. I keep the same slow pace, just circling, feeling all her muscles flex and tighten as her orgasm builds, as she tries to fight my grip, as she aches to grind herself into me, guide me, force my fingers where she wants them, how she wants them.

When she's all wound up and each one of her muscles is taut beyond their natural boundaries, I relent, settling on her clit and pressing hard and fast against her. Her moans are lovely and shrill, and if I wasn't here in the room with her, I'd be thinking someone was committing a crime. Her face contorts and twists as if she is in pain, and my cock aches at the sight of her. All the tension leaks out of her body as she explodes all over my fingers. The fight drains from her and suddenly she is dead weight as she giggles and pants, her eyes clamped shut as if she is in a different plane of existence.

I wait for her to open her eyes and for some of the tension to creep back into her body before I release her. I walk over to the bed and strip down my pants and boxers in one swift move. Then chuck off my shirt. Her hazy eyes trace over my body and her face lights up.

"Come here."

Her breath is still uneven and her steps shaky as she makes her way to me. She reaches for me, but I step out of her reach and sit on the edge of the bed. She comes closer, and I can see what she's thinking, but I have other ideas.

Before she can straddle me, I stop her and grapple with my savage need to get her on her knees and put her mouth to good use. I remind myself that I have all night. "Turn around."

She pouts for a second before she does, and I grip her hips backing her up so that her ass is in perfect alignment with my face. "Pull off your dress."

She looks at me over her shoulder before gripping the crumpled hem and pulling the dress over her head letting it fall at her feet. "You are beautiful," I say. And I mean it. She has a lovely hourglass shape and long straight hair that falls almost halfway down her back, not to mention that perfect fucking ass that I can barely take my eyes off.

My fingers trace the column of her back, just halfway up, and goosebumps erupt all over her skin. They trail down and my hand caresses her sweet plump ass cheeks. I dip them into her soaked pussy a few times before pulling out and making my way to her little asshole. "Tell me, Margot." I start to push a finger into her hole as I feel it clamp around me. My cock swells in excitement. "Have you ever been fucked in the ass?"

"Yes." She looks back at me again, and her face wears that strange expression between confidence and uncertainty.

My finger dips in and out of her tight little hole, and fuck if I'm not going stir crazy. "Did you like it?"

"Yes." Her clipped response has me giddy, and I push in a second finger, delighting in her sweet, surprised gasp.

"Good. Because I'd like to fuck your ass, Margot." My fingers stretch her out slowly; I'm nothing if not meticulous and patient with everything I do.

She doesn't respond but her body does for me, in the way her wet pussy glistens and drips onto her inner thighs, and the way she doesn't realise that she is moving into my touch, sucking my fingers deeper into her.

"Do you have any lube?" I throw out the question. She's booked a room looking for sex; I'm making an educated guess.

"Yes." I look up at the ceiling and thank whatever gods might still be listening to me. Not that I would have stopped if she said no, but let's be honest, it will be much better for the both of us if she actually enjoys it while I sodomise her.

"Go get it and be quick about it." I slap her ass and watch her take hurried little steps across the room where her handbag landed. She bends over to pick it up, and I get an eyeful of her holes, and fuck me they are gorgeous. I tear my eyes away so that I don't come all over myself.

I reach for my jeans and grab a condom from a pocket, tear the foil and slip it on just as she hands me a small travel-size bottle of lube. She came prepared. "Turn around."

She turns slowly, her gaze sweeping over my face with something akin to longing. I don't know if she wants kissing and cuddling, and to be honest, as I lather my cock with lube, I don't care. I am consumed with the thought of being inside her.

I grip her hips and pull her backwards and down. Lining the head of my cock up with her entrance, I guide her movements. She slides down and my tip nudges inside, and oh fuck she is so tight as she clamps around me. My forehead falls onto her smooth back as I hold her there, groaning against her.

I push her up again, hold for a few beats then let her slide down again. My tip back inside her, but only slightly more. I repeat this, listening to her sharp intake of breaths and feeling her hole expand around me, taking me in before I finally let her sink all the way down, and then I am inside her ass to the fucking hilt, and fuck she is tight. I can't help the snarl that rips from my mouth without me meaning to make a sound.

When I feel like she is settled, I snake my hands around her; one gripping her hip to keep her steady, the other curling around her neck, fingers locking beneath her jaw. I use my grip to force her head up, arching her back, driving her further down onto me. Her tight ass closing around my hard cock. My teeth bury themselves into her shoulder, and she whimpers as they clamp down.

Releasing her hip, my fingers make their way to her clit. She is so sensitive, her body shivers at the touch. She tries to struggle against the discomfort, only making me swell inside her, wanting more. I chuckle as my grip on her throat tightens. "Ride my cock, Margot."

Her hands land on my thighs and dig in for purchase as she starts to roll her hips while my fingers dance around her clit and my grip tightens around her throat. The flex of her neck making me harder, more excited as I keep pulling her back and down.

Her heart thunders—the pounds crashing against my hammering chest. Her fingers dig into my thighs as she gasps, trying to force air into her burning lungs. Her laboured breathing slows down her movements, so I let up just a little, allowing her to suck in two lungfuls of air before I tighten my grip again.

She keeps riding me. Anchored on my cock, I meet her

movements, pounding into her. My hands controlling the angle of her body, tightening around her throat. I love watching her face change a shade of dark red and the way the frantic panic sets in as she tries to pry herself off me. It just makes me harder as she whimpers, and it comes out like an unladylike gag. She chases air while at the same time chasing the pleasure my fingers promise her clit, and my cock just keeps swelling inside her as I watch her unde-cided, not knowing what she wants more.

Her hands drop to the side, the fight seeping from them as she wordlessly begs for air. Every muscle in her neck ripples beneath my hand as I release enough for her to gulp in a few more deep breaths before clamping down again.

Her breaths are short, small gasps—her fingers dig into my thighs, but she doesn't tap out or try to pry my fingers away. I leave her dripping pussy and capture a nipple in my fingers and pull—hard. A mangled cry falls from her closed-up throat and shoots right to my cock.

Her hands rake over my thighs trying to find somewhere to hold as I smash into her. Every inch of her trembles above me, her face blooming with crimson as the fight falls away from her hands again. I let up just enough for her to gasp for another breath before I slam into her again and close my fingers around her throat, watching the tears pooling at the corner of her eyes.

Her whole body clenches down around me and heat shoots through my body and collects in my ball sack. I come hard and fast. Everything below my belly button clenches painfully hard as if there was a battering ram being put to my body, but there is no pain, only pleasure.

An otherworldly shriek brings me half back just to watch as Margot convulses on top of me then collapses the last inch onto my chest.

I fall back onto the bed and catch my breath, my cock

growing limp inside her and slipping out. I don't know when she climbs off me, but she ends up on the bed, her ankles by my face as she lays catching her breath.

I get up and go to the bathroom, discarding the used condom and splashing cold water on my face. When I get back, I find her still lying on the bed. I like her. She looks like Guernica; like she's been torn apart and put back together again. I smile as she heaves another breath making her little titties move around.

If I was closer, I'd sink my teeth into them.

She stretches and unwinds herself then covers herself with the sheet. It's a lovely sight—a woman's body covered in a sheet like that—you know exactly what's underneath and yet all the beauty is hidden under a thin, pure, white layer of fabric.

"So," her voice yanks me out of my thoughts, "What's your real name?"

I cock an eyebrow at her. "What do you mean? It's Mark."

"It's not."

"You know then?"

"Of course I know. For one, the real Mark was called Scott, and he called me five minutes before I walked into the hotel to cancel on me, but I was already dressed and made up, and I paid for the fucking room, so I didn't want to go home. So, I walked around for a while till I saw you. You were cute, and I thought we could have a few drinks." She winks at me. "This was an unexpected bonus." Her face breaks into a shy sweet smile, so unsuited to her devilish nature. My cock twitches back to life.

"So who the hell is Mark?"

"I don't know." She shrugs. "You look like a Mark."

I scoff at her remark. "So, if you knew I wasn't him, why did you come upstairs with me?"

"You played along. You were kind, handsome and funny, and you told me you had the tools to fix my dishwasher."

"So basically, you took advantage of my plumbing skills?" I bring a hand to my heart in mock shock.

"Well..." She bites down on her lower lip, sucking it in. And I know we're about to go for round two and I'm finally going to put those lips to good use.

I lean back on the small dining table, my hands gripping the edge, testing the sturdiness. I have a feeling Margot is about to get intimately acquainted with it. "Still, you took a chance. How do you know I'm not some kind of serial killer?"

"You don't look like a serial killer." She shrugs and falls back onto her back, the sheet falling away from her breast showing off the bronzed skin and her dark right nipple.

"Oh? And what do they look like?"

She frowns for a second as she thinks about it. "No idea, evil maybe."

I laugh. "That's very... descriptive."

"Well, they'd be different."

"How so?"

"Well, for one, they kill you."

"Ah, fair point." I wink at her and look at the red finger marks that decorate her throat like lights on a Christmas tree. I wonder how she will explain that away when they change colour and bruise in the morning. "Now come here."

3

ROOM #871 - THE GIRL IN THE BLUE DRESS

Bella

The bar is full, as I knew it would be; a far cry from my empty apartment and emptier heart. I bite the inside of my cheek, reminding myself I wasn't going to think about that tonight; about *him*, about my life in tatters. The way his ass was in the air fucking that girl in our bed after ten years... after he told me he still loved me... after he asked me to stay.

Fuck him. Tonight, I'm not someone's broken vessel, a fractured broken thing. Tonight, I am a princess and I dressed up like one. So what if I am slightly over the top in my cocktail dress, and showing off a little too much skin and wearing the kind of make-up only supermodels wear? Tonight, I will be a queen in my own right and forget everything.

I call for the barman. His dark blue eyes take me in and flash with desire. I smile; this is the effect I want to have on everyone tonight. What I deserve tonight is to be worshipped.

"What can I get you?" he asks.

"A Shirley Temple please."

"Would you like a kinky Shirley Temple?" he asks me, and I lean in.

"What makes it kinky?"

"The way you drink it." He winks at me, and a warm shudder slides down to my belly as he pushes away to make my drink. I see him reaching up for a pink liquor labelled 'Kinky' from a top shelf, and a wave of disappointment washes over me. Maybe I was secretly hoping that I would make that drink more than it could be of I drank it just right.

Scanning the room, my gaze lands on a blackjack table. Three men sit at it, each studying the cards laid on the table before them. The bartender places my drink down, and I thank him before I pay and take a sip. The alcohol hits me and burns my throat, harsh liquid fire that runs and settles in my belly, flaming the anger and disillusion already burning inside me, but I am determined to take it and turn it into courage. Tonight, I'll be bold and adventurous. I will not be regular old 'Isi', that first part of my name that clings to me like a newborn child, innocent and pure. Tonight, I want to be 'Bella', that other part of me. A darker more curious part that isn't afraid and isn't timid and can do whatever the fuck she wants.

I order a second drink as I down my first; if I am going to pull off this shit, I'm going to need a little more courage, and where better to find it than at the bottom of a cocktail glass.

While the bartender makes my drink, I spot a man across the bar from me, his broad shoulders suggest that he is tall, his wild brown hair is untamed, and he sprouts a six o'clock shadow on his angular jaw.

He smiles at me, tipping his glass towards me, and I do the same. He stands, his eyes locked on mine, and I feel like my night is about to begin with this perfect stranger when a woman in a tight black dress cuts him off and they begin talking. I let out a small puff. *Maybe not.*

Shaking off my disappointments, I make my way to the unoccupied chair at the blackjack table and stand for a minute watching the three players. The one on the far right is exceedingly obese, his body sags around the chair on which he sits. The one in the middle is a short, lanky fellow, who keeps combing a hand through his silver hair and adjusting his glasses. The one on the left is tall, his jet-black hair is combed perfectly to one side and his stark, sharp jaw is peppered with a day's growth of hair.

"Is this seat taken?" I ask.

The man flashes me a quick look, his deep blue eyes flicker up and down my body appreciatively before he gestures to the empty seat.

"Be my guest." He has a dark pensive voice tinged in a delicious accent, and it wraps around me like hot liquid honey—silky and sweet—and pools somewhere between my thighs. I squirm at the incidental sensation. The man smirks at my side as I slide into the seat and squeeze my legs together.

The dealer sets aside the burn card and begins to deal. We each sit with two cards before us; I have two tens and a nervous stomach. The first guy asks for a hit and is a bust, the second stands, the handsome man next to me has a ten and a nine, and the house stands at 18. I stare at my pair of tens.

"What will the lady do?"

"The lady will split." The man beside me answers before I have a chance, and every tiny hair on my body stands at the command in his voice. Somehow, it's like he's not even talking about my pair of cards.

I nod at the dealer who still waits for my approval. Bella

is a chance-taker, she will take this split and see what happens.

"Good girl," the man beside me says in appreciation, and our eyes lock for a lingering moment. The dealer deals out two more cards. The swell of pride in my chest from his praise is quickly drowned out by elation as the dealer places a ten and a jack on my pair. A blackjack and a twenty and suddenly he's pushing a bunch of plastic coins my way, and four sets of eyes study me curiously.

I shriek in delight as the man next to me smirks at my antics. Whatever, tonight is about celebrating and being real, not about letting others judge me. That includes this man right here, even if his jaw is sharp enough to slice paper.

I collect my money, gathering it into two, neat, identical piles. The man eyes me as I do this, and we all wait for the dealer to reset and deal our new hand.

The dealer deals, and already everyone is looking in better shape than I am. A three and a two sit in front of me and mock my last victory. At my turn I tell the dealer to hit me—another three. I sigh pathetically and ask for a fourth card. When the dealer gives me a ten, my odds seem infinitely better, but not when I look around the table; better —but only...*ish*.

"Ask him for another," the man next to me says, except he isn't really suggesting it but commanding me to do it. I look into his dark blue eyes and hold his gaze. Bella isn't the kind of person who takes commands, she is bold and daring and can make up her own damn mind, but something about this man's voice and how it slides under my skin and sets me on fire makes me want to do anything he says.

I inhale, close my eyes, and when I let out my breath, I ask the dealer for another card. The ace of spades sits at the end of the five-card row, and not only am I not out, I win again, big.

"Good girl," the man next to me says again.

"My name is Bella," I finally say. I haven't been a girl in a long time, even though the way he says it makes my spine shiver and my body heat.

"And you can call me Ethan, for now."

For now? What the fuck does that mean? I nod and set my winnings in four perfectly even piles.

"You should go get yourself a drink," he says, and again it feels like far more than a suggestion.

I want to protest, but the idea of somehow disappointing him with my refusal makes me shift uncomfortably in my seat.

"Don't worry, Bella, I'll keep your seat warm." The way he says it makes my underwear want to burst into flames.

I slide off my seat feeling the pool of wetness in my underwear as I do, and grateful to have a reprieve from Ethan's stare and presence. I make my way back to the bar where the same barman spots me and winks. I smile and hold up a finger, and he's reaching for the red vodka liquor before I even get to the bar.

When I do, I don't notice the man who's holding two drinks in his hands, and I narrowly miss him. In his attempt to save his alcohol, he pulls away too quickly and both his hands get covered in booze.

"Shit," he hisses.

"I'm sorry," I start, and when he looks up, I recognise him; he's the man I thought was making his way over to me, before he left to sit down with the woman in the black dress. I spot her across the room at a table typing away on her phone.

"It's fine," he says and smiles as he recognises me, setting the spilt drinks on the bar.

"Oh, I really am so sorry, let me replace those."

"No, it's fine, I should have been watching where I was going."

"You should have, are you sure you don't have a drinking problem?" I make a point to look at both his drinks, knowing perfectly well he bought one for himself and one for his date.

A slow smile creeps across his face. His smile is sweet, and wholesome and Bella wants to flirt with this man. He doesn't make me feel so unnerved like Ethan does. There's something very calming about him. "You should be careful with that joke, it's an antique."

"You wouldn't know a joke if it bit you on the ass." I gasp as the words leave my mouth. Isi would never talk this way. Isi is timid and polite. But Bella....

The man leans in closer, setting my heart fluttering in my chest. "If someone was going to bite me on the ass, she had better have bought me dinner first."

I would love to buy him dinner. Not tonight of course but... I open my mouth to ask for his number, maybe throw out another cheeky reply, when the barman places our drinks down and asks for his money. The man pulls out his credit card and holds it between two fingers, all the while his eyes remain locked on mine.

I cross my hands over my chest. "I said I'd get the drinks."

"And I said it was fine," he says as the barman returns his card.

"Thank you." I reach for my Shirley Temple and realise our time has come to an end once again. His date is staring up at us. "It was nice to meet you...?"

"Dean." His smile is boyish and charming, and I wonder what sort of night we could have had together if he wasn't on a date with the girl in the black dress.

"It was nice to meet you, Dean, I'm Isi."

"Have a great night, Isi." He tips his drink over to me, still smiling, and makes his way back to his date.

As I make my way back to the blackjack table, I half wonder why I introduced myself to Dean as Isi. Why I prefer he knows me as someone more homely. Maybe it's the way he makes me feel safe and calm, while Etan makes me feel like I am walking a tightrope and I'm unsure he would offer me a hand if I fall.

When I reach my seat, Ethan has a dark agitated look about him. I'm not sure why it should matter, seeing as I only just met him thirty minutes ago, but it does. He seems disappointed, annoyed even, and for some reason that makes me feel a little disappointed too. I shake off the feeling as I slide back onto my seat and the dealer deals a new hand.

"How was your drink?" he asks.

"It was... Good." It *was* good; it made me feel more relaxed again, freer, and the chat with Dean made me smile and made butterflies flourish in my stomach; a sensation I didn't know I could feel again. Not this soon. I put it down to my drinks. I haven't had this much alcohol in I don't even know how long, but it's making me bolder and braver, and a hum of happiness lies beneath the surface of my skin.

We play a few more rounds. Between the alcohol, Ethan's constant unrelenting and slightly unnerving attention, not to mention lady luck, I'm having a great night.

Ethan stands up and slicks a hand over his suit, pulling down the slight creases that have formed while he sat down. He closes a single button on his suit jacket and looks at me. "Are you ready?"

"For what?" I glance up at him, and he lets out an irritated sigh as if I am missing something obvious.

"To retire." He cocks his head to the right and raises an

eyebrow. The movements are deliberate, and the message is clear.

I swallow hard. A handsome stranger is asking me, no, *telling* me that he wants to take me upstairs to his room. Isi would never dare to do anything like this, but Bella? Bella has grand notions of passion, of this man pinning her against the door of the room and kissing her hard, possessing her with his mouth and later with his body. Erasing every shred of the last ten miserable years with orgasm after orgasm. I slide off my chair and give a slight nod. Ethan returns the gesture and offers me his arm. I lace mine into his, and he guides us away from the noise and the lights to the elevator bank that will take us to the hotel above.

"Where are we going?" I ask, but he ignores my question.

I wait a few more beats as he pushes the button, remaining silent.

"What do you do for a living?"

He gives me that same look that he did at the table a few moments ago, like maybe I am missing something, and I bite my lower lip, sealing all my other questions inside.

He doesn't talk. His silence is stark and brooding and slithers around me, but it's not cold or scary, it's intriguing and mysterious, and all I want is more of it so I can find out what lies behind it when he finally starts to speak. It sparks my curiosity and ignites something heated and dangerous low in my belly.

The elevator chimes, and the door slides open. The first wave of fantasy consumes me. I want to walk into the elevator with that man and throw myself at him; allow him to pin me to the cold mirror at the back and let him steal my breath away with his mouth. Instead, four young kids push their way into the elevator with us. Two are barely standing, the other two, who glare at each other as if they want to kill one another, are clearly trying to get them back to the safety of their rooms. They reek of alcohol, and disappointment chews its way through me.

Ethan stands at the back of the elevator unperturbed by the intruders. The elevator stops again, and a man in jeans and a T-shirt walks inside. He ignores all of us as we continue up. The kids get off first. The silent man travels a few more stories with us before he reaches his floor and leaves us behind. When we are finally alone, Ethan remains standing at the back of the elevator, eyeing me slowly with his deep blue eyes as if nothing has changed. I let out a small puff of disappointment and look at my hands, feeling his eyes on me.

When the elevator comes to a smooth stop, he waits for me to take his offered arm again, and he leads us out to the corridor before taking out a key card and opening a door. He holds it open for me. I take in a long breath knowing I can still be Isi, knowing I can still back out at any time, knowing this isn't something I would do. Then I cross the threshold and hear the door close behind me.

"You're not what I thought you'd be. The agency said you'd have dark hair."

I spin around to the sound of his voice and see him standing near the door in the shadowy part, his eyes raking slowly over my body. "The agency?"

He nods. "Have they given you the instructions I sent?"

I shake my head having no idea what he might be refer-ring to.

He runs a hand over his chin and his mouth stretches into a thin line. He doesn't seem happy. "It's okay. We'll just work with what we have. Go into the bathroom and get ready for me."

I stare at him. "What do I need to do?"

"What do I need to do, *Sir*."

"Excuse me?"

He lets out a short sharp breath. "*Sir*. That is how you will refer to me. Understand?"

"Yes... Sir."

"Good girl." He seems relieved as his eyes lock onto my lips for a few beats. "Now go get ready."

"How... Sir?"

His lips twitch in a quick smile. He seems pleased.

"I want you to take everything off but your underwear and put your hair up in pigtails. Braided."

I stare at him for a long moment. This isn't what I expected when I followed him up to the room.

"When you come back out there will be no more talking, only Sir gets to talk, so he can tell you what he wants you to do and how. You will not question Sir and you will do what you are told. Do you understand?"

"Yes, Sir."

"Good, then why are you still here? Sir doesn't like repeating himself."

"Yes, Sir," I say in a shaky voice and make my way to the lavish bathroom. It's big and ornate and no expense has been spared when designing this place. It's unlike any hotel room I've ever been to before. Then again, Isi has never been in a penthouse before. Isi has never real been anywhere. Bella is about to change that.

My fingers shake as I slowly undo the zip on my dress and let it fall away from my body. My heart shivers in my chest as it pools at my feet, and I step out of the material, setting it neatly aside. I'm not wearing a bra; the corset of the dress was holding me in, and automatically I bring my hands up to cover my breasts, despite being alone in the room. I'm left in my underwear as I stare at my reflection and gulp a few lungfuls of air before I start to run my fingers through my hair, brushing out the few knots. Splitting my hair into two parts, I grab the first and start twisting the strands into a braid, staring at my reflection.

What the hell am I doing? This isn't what I want. Is it? I want passionate kissing and a man to slowly undo the zip of my dress, to gasp as he drinks in my body and slowly move me to the bed. For his hands to carefully and gently glide along my skin, to sink inside me and erase the last few days. To make me feel whole again, even if it's just a lie. Just a moment.

But this man, Ethan—he isn't like that. He doesn't want to indulge in slow romantic notions. And yet. I'm still braiding my hair.

This isn't what I want.

Is it?

When I'm done, I take one more look at myself in the mirror. My skin hums, adrenalin floods my veins with giddy anticipation and my heart thunders inside my chest. But all of it is drowned out by my too loud breathing in this too large bathroom. I grab the doorknob, promising myself I can leave if I hate it. I cover up my nudity and step into the room.

I find Ethan standing in the middle of the room. His torso is bare, showing off a six-pack, his dress pants hanging loosely off his hips where the bones protrude just slightly, creating a delicious V I can't help but stare at. A dark length of hair carves his belly in two and vanishes beyond the line of his boxers.

He takes a short sharp breath as he sees me. "Did I say you can look at me?"

I shake my head.

"Speak."

"No," I choke out.

"No, *Sir*," he corrects.

"No, Sir," I mimic, then drop my eyes to the floor where my toes bury themselves into the soft carpet.

"Did I say you can cover yourself?"

"No, Sir." I swallow the lump that rises in my throat.

We stand in a short silence. He doesn't move. He waits for me. I squeeze my eyes shut and find the will to move my hand away, letting it fall from my breasts.

"My toy is very beautiful," he says, his voice a little deeper than it was a second ago.

I hear him move, and my body shivers as his hand clasps around my wrist and he leads me towards the wall, faces me towards it and places my hand on the cold surface. "Both hands will remain on the wall," he instructs.

I do as he says.

"Good girl." He praises me as he urges my feet farther apart with his own. "If you make a sound or move your hands, I will spank your arse."

I gasp, all the breath leaving my lungs in a wheezing sound like a balloon leaking air, and turn to look at his face, his eyes burning and narrow. Shit, I've broken the rules already. I turn back to the wall.

"Good girl." He hums, and that singular sound trickles through me like hot chocolate sauce on ice cream.

I feel his gaze burning a trail along my back, down to my ass and the length of my legs.

"Beautiful," he says. But he doesn't come near me. All I feel is the warmth of his eyes along my naked body.

"Does my toy have a safe word?"

"Safe word?"

"Something she won't easily forget. If she wants Sir to stop."

Why would I want him to stop? I shiver at the thought. "Purple?" The colour of the underwear that was thrown on the floor of *our* bedroom, while he fucked her in *our* bed. I won't forget my safe word, ever. And nothing will get me colder and dryer then those memories.

"Are you asking me or telling me?"

"It's purple, Sir."

"Good girl."

I sense his movement a second before I feel a single finger slither down my back tracing the bones of my spine. I shiver. Electricity crackles over my skin, and my body erupts in goosebumps. Heat rushes to my pussy and a pool of moisture settles in my underwear. My skin is on fire, and he's only used a single finger.

"Very receptive," he murmurs as if to himself, then his hand trails back up and slides down again. He grips my underwear and pulls up, forcing the fabric between my pussy and ass cheeks.

I hiss at the sudden unexpected force of it after his gentle stroking, and he pulls up further, the fabric pushing my throbbing clit.

"Is my toy wet?" he asks.

"Yes, Sir."

He makes a low sound that rumbles through me and makes my body pulse as his free hand slides along my shoulder and traces the length of my neck. "How wet?"

"Very wet, Sir," I say, feeling heat sting my cheeks and ears.

"Not wet enough then," he says, and his hand rounds my neck and closes slowly around my throat.

He doesn't squeeze, just lets his hand rest there letting me know he's in charge while his other hand drags up my belly and finds a breast. I gasp at his touch and he murmurs. His fingers explore me. He pulls, then pinches, and I cry out. The pain is momentary and the pleasure that follows sends a thrill to my pussy. I have a desperate need to clench my thighs.

"Shhh, you're not to make another sound." His dark voice creeps in my ear and his hot breath licks my shoulder.

His hand is back at my breast. He keeps teasing my nipple that grows harder with each touch, his fingers expertly tugging and pulling, his thumb rolling over the sensitive flesh, wreaking havoc on my body.

I push into him; his hard cock nudges my back as I do.

"Tsk tsk. You're a naughty toy. Don't move." It's a dark and menacing warning.

I whimper; my body needs more. *I* need more.

"What did I tell you about making a sound?"

"But—"

"And now you're speaking?"

His hands fall away, and his heat is gone as he steps away from me. I suck in a breath, closing my eyes.

The smack comes hard and fast, the sound reverberating in the silent room. I shriek, my eyes flying open and my body stiffening as I feel the sting on my ass. My hands fall away from the wall, and I nurse the sudden pain. My eyes catch his.

He studies me for a second, his deep searing eyes burning. "I didn't say you could move your hands or touch your arse."

I open my mouth to apologise then shut it immediately as one of his brows quirks up.

I bite my lower lip instead, keeping my words at bay and let my eyes fall back to the floor. Inside my chest, my heart is a wild animal.

Despite the pain in my ass, my body is screaming, and my pussy is aching with need. I'm drenched, and we've only just started. What have I gotten myself into?

"Hands on the wall," he instructs with a steady voice.

I do as he says and wait. Feeling his eyes back on me.

"You've not been listening to Sir, and now I'll have to punish you. Tell me you understand."

"Yes, Sir."

"Good girl."

"I'm going to smack your arse now, four times. And if you move, I'll have to smack it again. Do you understand?"

"Ye... Yes, Sir." I swallow the lump in my throat and brace myself against the wall as terror lights up all my nerve endings.

"Good girl."

The slaps come in quick succession, two on each cheek. I bite down the cries that want to fall from my lips and wonder what the fuck I'm doing. I'm a fucking educated thirty-five-year-old woman, what the hell am I doing letting a man spank me like a misbehaving little girl? But even as the words filter through my brain, my body is radiating in ways I had never imagined. Sir is smoothing his hand slowly over my heated ass cheeks.

"Sir's toy took her punishment well," he croons, and a flush of pride fills me. Totally at odds with these feelings I should be having of shame and humiliation. But I feel none of that, just eager anticipation for what comes next.

I don't have to wait long. Ethan stands behind me once more, one hand back at my throat, the other back to the same nipple, making my other one crave his touch. He torments me slowly, his fingers peeling off my sanity one stroke at a time.

I'm desperate for more and yet I can't tell him, can't beg him, can't move my body. He's taken away all my ways to communicate, and I hate him for it.

"How wet is my toy now?" he finally asks, giving me an outlet.

"Soaked," I croak, not recognising my own voice.

"Good," he says as his hand leaves my nipple and slides

down my belly to my underwear. His fingers sink into the fabric and slide easily into my aching pussy. He groans in appreciation.

"You are soaked," he confirms as his thumb slowly begins to circle my clit. "This pussy is going to be nice and sore tomorrow." He leans in, nipping at my shoulder. I inhale a shuddering breath. "But don't worry I'll kiss it and make it all better."

A little whimper falls from my lips at his promise, and my eyes grow wide as his hand vanishes.

Fuck.

No.

Yes.

"My toy doesn't follow instructions very well, does she?"

I don't answer in fear of breaking more of his rules.

"Two spanks this time," he says and doesn't wait before he delivers two swift smacks to my already stinging ass. My body is set alight, and I swallow down the whimpers that want to tumble from my mouth.

"Next time it will be four. Does my toy understand?"

"Yes, Sir."

"Will my toy behave?"

"Yes, Sir," I promise, proud of myself that my hands are still glued to the wall as they should be.

"Good girl," he says, and once again he's back behind me, his hand at my throat and the other back to my nipple.

I want to cry. I want him back at my clit, and yet he remains on that one single nipple till my eyes sting with tears and my body is frustrated. I bite down hard to keep my desperation locked inside me, my breaths coming out in long hard pants.

When he feels that he's punished me enough, his hands slide along my belly once more and his fingers once again start at my clit; long torturous circles that have me needing to moan and move. I'm gasping for air and trembling madly and feel like I might be going out of my mind. I need so much more, yet he's revelling in my silent torment.

"You're such a good toy," he whispers into my ear as his hand slips out of my underwear and his fingers appear at my mouth. He pushes in, and I let him breach the seam of my lips. "Taste yourself; clean Sir's fingers."

I'm desperate for something, and I eagerly suck at his fingers as he pushes them in and out of me. My tongue savouring the musky flavour.

"Does my toy taste good?"

"Yes, Sir, very good." I'm surprised at myself. How easily I've succumbed to him, to this. I've never even thought of what it would be like to taste myself; the idea crude and indecent, and yet here I am lapping at his fingers.

His fingers leave my mouth with an audible pop before he yanks on one of my pigtails, turning my face to his. His eyes are hooded and dark and his stark jaw clenched, his neck corded. His mouth closes over mine and he kisses me —a long, hungry kiss.

"You taste delicious," he says in a pleased hum before releasing my pigtail and allowing my face to turn back to the wall and my stupid pride to swell in my chest. I like that he likes me. I like that he likes my taste. Patrick stopped telling me he loved me years ago. Let alone anything else.

Ethan's hands slide down my sides, then grab my underwear, bunching it up and pulling up again, forcing the fabric against my aching clit. I bite down my sounds.

"Sir wants to finger-fuck your beautiful pussy," he says gruffly, and heat rises from my chest, coating my face. My entire body tingles and pulses at his words. No one has ever spoken to me like that. In my ten years with Patrick, he's not once uttered the word pussy, let alone told me what he wanted to do to it.

He releases the grip on my underwear, and I miss the sensation instantly. Ethan slides the underwear down my legs and groans. His deep rumble shivers through me, and my aching pussy pulses with need.

"Bend over for me, beautiful," he rumbles, and I comply, my heart beating like a hammer. My body just does what it's told, my brain no longer part of the conversation.

"Rest your head on your arms. And don't move again."

I brace myself against the wall.

"God, your holes are fucking perfect." His voice sounds almost strained.

Ethan falls to his knees and helps me release the underwear from my ankles before spreading me wide again. I'm totally aware of his face by my asshole and pussy, and a myriad of emotions swim inside me. Excitement, fear, embarrassment, power; it's all intoxicating. One of his hands runs along my inner leg, making its way up along my thigh before he sinks two fingers inside me.

"So fucking wet," he says. "I want to see your juices running down onto my hand. I want you to coat Sir's hand with your pussy juice. Can you do that for Sir?"

"Yes." I moan. Hoping I can. Wishing I can. Not sure I want to.

"Yes, who?"

"Yes, Sir."

"Good girl. But Sir doesn't want to have to remind you again." I feel the sting of his words and my ass burns with memory. "Sir is going to finger-fuck you hard till his hand is covered in your wetness and then he'll finger-fuck your arse."

At his words, my breath hitches and my asshole clenches. I hear the deep chuckle as his teeth graze my ass cheek. His fingers start to move inside me, his thumb on my clit. He slides in and out of me in a steady rhythm.

My legs start to shake, and my breaths come out in sharp, shallow pants. I'm close and I know he knows it because he pulls out of me and then slams three fingers into me. I moan with pleasure, with surprise, with delight, then bite my lip. Fuck.

His fingers vanish before he stands up and lands four devastating smacks onto my ass.

He falls back to his knees without a word as my body digests the new sensation. I'm overwhelmed.

"Not. A. Sound," he commands as he falls back onto his knees. His fingers sink into me once again, and I bite the inside of my cheek.

"I love the sight of your red arse." He pulls his fingers out of my pussy and repositions them so that one rests at the entrance of my asshole. He slides it in gently, his fingers slick with my juices. My breathing falters, and I clamp around him in surprise before finding myself pushing into him.

"Don't move!"

I will myself to stand still as he pushes deeper still.

"Fuck, your body is amazing."

I thrill at the reverence of his voice, and any self-conscious thought about my body evaporates by the awed way he appreciates it.

His fingers start to work me, ploughing in and out in a maddening rhythm. I'm close again as his thumb strums my clit, and my ass burns and my pussy clenches. I can't catch my breath. My awareness narrows to that tiny bundle of nerves between my legs throbbing under his endless assault.

"Please," I beg him, forgetting his rules, bypassing any consequences.

"Would my toy like to come for Sir?" he purrs, his fingers unrelenting.

"Yes. Please, Sir," I beg.

He pulls his fingers out of me and stands up. "Not yet. You come when your owner comes." I groan in mad frustration, my mind splintering. He pulls on one of my pigtails, pulling me away from the wall. I stand on shaky feet, straightening my strained back as he leads me to the bed.

"Get on your back and spread your legs wide for me."

I climb onto the bed, my body covered in a sheen of sweat, my ass burning, my pussy aching and needy.

I lie down on my back, but my legs won't open. I grind them together, chasing the empty sensation between them. I need to be filled, to be fulfilled.

"I said open," he says, grabbing my ankles, pulling them apart, exposing me. He's still in his pants, but I can see the bulge of his massive erection pushing against the fabric. I want him inside me. But he just stands there, completely in control, showing no indication that he's concerned with anything other than calming me down and winding me up.

His hands roll over his erection as his eyes take me in, hungry and hooded and full of dark desires. I've never felt so pretty or powerful as I do under the worshipping hands and ravenous eyes of this man.

"I want you to play with your pussy," he says, and I glare at him. My heart stutters. *What? What the fuck does that mean?*

When I don't move, he gives me the instructions I'm desperate for. "Run your fingers along the inside of your thighs."

I do as he says, and his gaze traces the slow journey my fingers make. My skin shivers at my touch. His tongue slips out of his mouth, and he moistens his lips. Heat radiates inside me as I imagine what his tongue might feel like on my pussy.

"Fuck you're beautiful," he groans, stroking his shaft

through the fabric of his pants. "Run your finger between your lips and tell me how wet you are."

Heat coats my skin as my fingers slide along my pussy. The light touch sends a thrill up my back, and my body erupts in goosebumps, my pussy aching for more. "Soaked, Sir." My voice shivers, unrecognisable to me.

"Soaked enough to push a couple of fingers into yourself?"

"Mmhmm."

"Good girl." His ferocious eyes glare down at my hands. "I want you to push two fingers inside yourself. Knuckle deep, then fuck yourself with them. Slowly."

I do as he says. The shame falls away from me as his gaze burns and he makes low noises deep in his throat. "You're such a good fucking toy," he says and nears the bed, flicking open the button of his dress pants and easing the zipper down. He lets them drop then shoves off his boxers, letting me have my first look at his massive cock. It's hard and swollen, the vein pulsing, and a drop of pre-cum coats the top. He glides over it with his thumb and rubs it over the head as he watches me. "So fucking beautiful," he says as he climbs onto the bed, on his knees, his body looming over me.

"Put your hands above your head," he commands, and I do as he says. A slow whimper leaks out of me as once again I am left needy and empty.

Once I am settled, he grabs my knees, pulling them up and puts pressure on them so that he has total control of my body as my back arches for him, begging to be touched. He smirks knowingly, lining himself up with my pussy and pushing inside me. But only the tip. We both groan at the intrusion, and I find myself trying to push against his hands so I can have more of him.

"Don't move," he growls as his tip remains inside me and

his thumb finds its way to my clit. He starts with slow agonising circles that test my sanity. I don't think I can take more of his torture. My body begins to shake, and the climax builds inside me again, pleasure just out of reach as he pulls out and away all at once and commands me to get onto my knees.

"I want to see all your holes," he says as he flips me over and pushes my legs into position, my body almost too weak to comply with his demands. "Hands at the top of the bed."

Tears sting my eyes as I bury my face into the pillow, wondering if this is what insanity feels like; a constant chasing for a feeling that never comes.

His hands run the length of my back before his teeth graze my ass cheeks. My body is burning, an avalanche of sensations and feelings I do not know if I can contain much longer.

He lines his cock up with my pussy and rests there. I try to push back, but his hand holds my lower back, keeping me in place and him in total control. I'm desperate to grind on something, but all I find is air.

"Tell me what you want, Bella."

"You." I groan into the pillow, my heart thrashing in my chest, my body screaming with want.

"Where?"

"You know where, Sir." I moan.

"If you don't tell me, you won't get what you want."

"You, Sir," I repeat through gritted teeth.

"Not good enough. Does my toy want Sir to fuck her?"

"Yes." It's a desperate admission.

"Then tell Sir what you want!" His tone is low and commanding, and it pulls the words from my mouth like a thread.

"I want your cock inside me."

"Reach down between your legs and rub your clit hard."

I do as he says, and a moment later, he pushes the tip of his cock into my pussy.

I cry out, my back bowing as he slides his hands towards my nipples and squeezes them hard.

Ethan pulls back out again, then pushes in a little deeper, repeating the move again and again.

"Fuck I love watching my cock slip in and out of you, coated in your wetness."

I'm gasping for air and trembling madly, and I feel like I might be going out of my mind as he finally pushes his entire length into me.

Slowly.

Purposefully.

"Please," I hear myself begging him.

"Please? What does my toy want?"

"Please, Sir, I want your cock inside me."

"Good girl. My toy will get what she wants." With one hand on the arch of my back, he pushes me downward then pushes his thumb into my ass.

I gasp at the intrusion, or maybe I moan, or maybe the noise is so foreign, so unfamiliar, it is a wild, feral thing that runs out of my mouth and escapes into the room.

Slowly, he builds up the pace. No more tip, but his entire length.

Sounds tumble out of me, uninhibited wild sounds that I've never heard myself make before as he grabs me by the hair and pulls my head back like he's riding me.

And I want him to. I want everything he has to give me.

"Is my toy ready to come?" His voice is no longer controlled but strained, coming through in harsh pants.

"Yes, Sir, please, Sir."

"Have you been a good girl?" he says as he pounds into me, quickening his pace, smashing into me hard and fast.

"Yes, Sir," I cry out in fervent desperation.

"Then you may come."

At his words, I unravel, overcome with sensations as a violent shockwave of pleasure ripples through me, wracking my body. I search for breath as my heart explodes in my chest and my eyes squeeze shut. Everything in the universe is a ball of violent pleasure.

Somewhere in the midst of my orgasm, I hear him tell me I have a beautiful cunt, a tight little pussy that he loves to fuck. He tells me I'm a good girl, a perfect toy, and his words obliterate me. I feel the tears come. I am so overwhelmed but still he pounds into me a few more times before his body turns rigid and his nails dig into my hips and he growls and grunts like an animal. My pussy throbs at the sound, erotic and splendid, and I wish I could bottle it and carry it with me.

Ethan hovers over me, and I feel the heat of his breath on my shoulder a beat before he lands a soft kiss on my skin. He tugs on my pigtail, forcing my head to his and slamming his mouth into me, kissing me hard; possessive, hungry, beautiful. He pulls away and sighs against my mouth, "You are a very good girl."

He releases me and falls onto his back, scooping me into his arms. "Are you okay?"

Am I? I feel like my brain has short-circuited, but I am okay. I am safe. I just feel good, emotional, overwhelmed, satisfied. "Yes," I say and grin up at him even as my tears sting my eyes.

"Good." He gives me a dark smile and releases me, then gets on his knees, "cause my toy needs to remember her place and clean my cock with her mouth."

My mouth falls open as he waits. His eyebrow quirks up, waiting for reply.

"I... I thought we were done." My voice feels small, and

my body feels exhausted; it wants to rest. I want to sleep cradled in his arms.

"What did Sir tell you earlier?"

I search my frazzled mind. Sir said a lot of things. He looks at my expression and helps me out. "I told you that your pussy will be nice and sore tomorrow, and that I plan on kissing it better."

I swallow the lump in my throat and flush at the arousal that ripples through my body.

"Is my toy's pussy sore?"

"No, Sir." But...

"And has Sir had a chance to kiss it better?"

"No, Sir."

He smirks. "Then you better start sucking."

4

ROOM #702 - WRONG NUMBER

Andi

The phone trills in the room, setting my heart fluttering and breaking through the moaning coming from the room next door. I've turned the TV on in a vain attempt to drown out the sounds, but it seems to have only spurred the woman on, and now she's crying even louder.

In truth, the noise pulls me out of my head, from the dark, empty void I've been sitting in. Tonight only proved to me for a final time how pathetic my existence really is, and how utterly alone I have become. Despite my publisher booking the banquet room and spending hundreds on advertising, promising my debut novel launch would be a massive success, I was forced to read out my speech in front of the five people who showed up. My voice shook the entire time, and was the voice of a defeated woman, one whose excitement had built up through the day, only to fizzle out into total humiliation.

When I finally snuck away, there were hundreds of uneaten hors d'oeuvres and rows of untouched wine glasses. Tonight was meant to be a dazzling affair; a launch into a career I've always chased and finally thought I'd broken into. Instead, it finally broke me. Even my own family members didn't show up. I ended up selling and signing two books; one to my publisher's daughter, the other to her mother. Humiliation feels like a thousand butterflies burning alive in your stomach.

The only consolation is that the publisher is paying for my room, and it has a minibar, which I have already half emptied.

The phone rings again and I set down my glass of gin and my toiletries bag. I look over at the bedside table where the phone rings for a third time.

I approach it and consider who would be calling me, and why? My publisher has my cell number and no one but her knows my room number. I take another step towards it and the shrill ring fills the room.

I lift the phone from the cradle and bring it to my ear. "Hello?" My voice sounds hoarse. I have been crying; I wonder if the caller can tell.

"Who is this?" a husky male voice on the other end questions me.

"Who is *this*? You called me," I state the obvious, bristling back at the intruder of my grief.

"You will earn my name if you are a good girl and do what you're told."

The answer irritates me but also sends a ripple of heat and curiosity along my body. I clear my throat. "I think you have the wrong room."

"I think you should talk less and listen more."

I gasp at the sharpness of his words and consider dropping the phone back into its cradle.

"Now, tell me what you're wearing."

I consider his words for a minute and study my reflection in the door-length mirror hiding the empty wardrobe. I could tell him the truth; my long ill-fitting tracksuit pants and t-shirt that I threw on after my shower, but for some reason, I don't. "I'm wearing a singlet and boy shorts," I hear myself saying.

He purrs into the phone, and it's a sexy sound that has my body reacting.

"That singlet needs to come off so I can put my mouth on your nipples."

There's a hunger in his voice that surprises me. Who the hell is this man? "You have the wrong number," I say again, but he ignores me.

"I said the singlet needs to go."

I consider my options. I can play along with this stranger on the phone, or I can hang up and go on with my pity party. I think about the razor waiting for me in the toiletries bag, the one that lays on the edge of the bed where I left it a moment ago.

"It's off," I say in a shaky voice, looking at myself fully dressed in the mirror.

"Good." His voice is deep and rich and hungry. "Tell me what colour your nipples are."

"No."

"You are being a very bad girl, and I'm running out of patience." There's a threat in his voice, a carnality that I don't quite know how to feel about. "Now tell me the colour."

I think about my breasts, I've never given much heed to the colour of my nipples. "I don't know."

"Figure it out."

It's an odd request but one that has me thinking about my body in a way I never have before. I rip off my T-shirt and look at my breasts in the mirror, focusing on my nipples. The more I look the harder they get, their hue darkening under my stare as heat skates along my body and desire flares between my legs.

"They're a dark pink, maybe like a dark rose." I shrug. I don't know how to describe their colour, but suddenly I wish I did know. Maybe I'd be a better writer if I did, maybe more people would have come tonight if I'd paid more attention to the details of things around me.

"That's very sexy." He hums in pleasure, his voice slicing through my thoughts and sending a flurry of heat to my cheeks. "I would love to graze my teeth over them."

I gasp. No one has ever spoken to me like this.

"Would you like that?" The voice on the phone is guttural and breathy.

"Yes," I whisper with a creaking voice.

"I know you would. Just before I put my mouth on it and suck it till it pops out. Then a quick look again before running my teeth across it. From one side to the other..."

I hear a soft pleasurable hum, and I'm shocked to realise it's me. I'm purring at his words, at the idea of this total stranger playing with my nipples. I think about the last time anyone had done that. It's been so long it feels like a lifetime ago, and even then, the experience was short-lived and barely worth remembering.

"Mmmm, you like that." I hear his smile on the other end of the line.

"Yes..." My voice has been hijacked by uncertainty and is hoarse and raw.

"Are your nipples sensitive?"

I remain silent, the voice on the other end of the line keeps pushing boundaries.

"I asked you a question." His voice clips, and my heart rattles in my chest.

"Yes."

"Yes, what?"

"They are sensitive, very sensitive."

"Are you touching them?"

Heat coats my skin. I look at myself in the mirror, frowning. But I question who the frown is for; the man on the other end, invading my privacy and seeking to know private things about me? Or me for being so severely wound up that I can't let go. What will happen if I allow his voice to invade my room and my body? We are two strangers colliding in a singular path that will veer off in another direction never to meet again. So why not? I silence the voices of my conscience and allow myself to be swept away and let go. Just once.

"I asked you a question." He's irritated again, but his voice doesn't carry a threat but a certain domineering quality that promises me he will have what he wants from me, he is certain of it. He isn't asking, he is simply telling me.

"Yes, I am touching them." And this time I do. I run my hands over my breasts, letting my fingers brush over my already hardened nipples. Goosebumps erupt across my flesh as I roll my thumb over one, then the other in turn.

"How does it feel?"

"Good."

"Just good?"

I shrug to myself, wondering what he wants me to say. It feels... erotic and strange, stimulating and confusing. A war rages between my brain and my body; this brain that is trained to believe what I am doing is wrong, forbidden, frowned upon. And yet my body responds, my thighs squeeze together as my fingers brush over my nipple again. And despite all the words that circulate in my head, I cannot seem to clutch to one singular one that encapsulates all that I feel in this moment—the simple obedience to a stranger on the phone to touch myself in the simplest of ways.

I remain silent, and he takes it as a cue to move on. "Are you wet?"

Yes, I am wet. The smooth timbre of his assured voice and the intrusive nature of it makes me feel like I have sprung a leak. My unused body blooming to life under this intruder's command. My mouth locks up and seals my words inside, if I could just write them down for him maybe then I could express myself. I have lived on paper for so long it's hard to be ripped from the pages and forced to partake in real life. Even if it feels strangely good. "Yes," I whisper and wish I was braver like some of the heroines I've written about.

"Wet enough to stick a finger inside yourself?"

My heart flutters in my chest, but I know it's shame rearing its ugly head. Yet, I already promised myself I would let go... "Yes."

"Good. Then do it."

My hand stutters across my chest where I'm still brushing it over my breasts. The woman from the next room is moaning again, begging. I don't know if it's for more or for less, but the thought of her getting fucked against our shared wall has my pussy clenching. I realise that I want to be that woman and that this voice on the phone can allow me that fantasy.

I fall onto the bed, settling myself and sliding my hand along my belly and into my pants, pushing under the fabric of my underwear and sliding along my wet pussy. I gasp.

"Good girl." He misinterprets my reaction, but it's okay. "How does it feel?"

Again with that fucking question I have no answer for. It feels like I've just woken up from a long fucking sleep. My body remembers echoes of being touched, but it's been neglected for too long, like every other area of my life. It feels fucking thrilling to touch myself again at the behest of a man. It feels incredibly hot and wet, I want to cry for all the time I've lost forgetting myself.

"You still haven't answered my question." He sounds displeased, cleaving through my thoughts with his dark smooth voice.

"It feels... amazing." I sigh as my finger still slides in and out of myself. My clit suddenly greedy after so many years of neglect already screaming for more.

There's a sound that he makes then, something feral and savage that sounds like a growl and it crawls from the earpiece and covers my entire body, sinking into my core as I shiver at the carnality of it. "Good, now take it out and taste it."

I freeze mid-motion. *What?*

"Don't think about it. Stop overthinking my instructions and do what you are told. Pull your finger out of your pussy and put it in your mouth." His voice is gruff and commanding.

My brain blinks off for a few seconds as if rebooting, and without much thought, I do what I am told. I push my finger into my mouth and suck it clean, tasting myself.

"How do you taste?"

I buy myself time sucking on my finger, the sweet, musky flavour of me coating my tongue, but I don't want to use those words, they feel... unsexy, and suddenly I realise that maybe I want to sound sexy. I settle for "delicious", and I am rewarded with a long purr of pleasure that sends heat trickling inside me and expanding through every inch of me.

"Did you like that?"

"Yes." Lying seems pointless.

"Good, now, put your fingers back inside your pussy and fuck yourself until you come."

"I..." *What?* Who the fuck does this? Who calls another person and listens to them come on the phone? Is this what the world has been doing while I have had my nose stuck in a computer screen creating worlds and passions that were nothing like this crude reality?

"Stop overthinking," he admonishes my stunned silence, and my body refuses to pay any heed to the sense that my brain is trying to feed it.

My fingers pop out of my mouth and slide along my body before sinking back into my damp underwear, where they brush over my clit. I moan unintentionally and almost hear the smile on the other end of the line.

"Good girl," he says in his smooth, dark timbre, and my body shivers.

It's been so long even the slightest touch has me melting under my own fingers, accentuating my building pleasure. He remains silent for a few moments, listening to me breathe, listening to my breath quicken and the soft silent whimpers I try to bite down. Each time I build myself up my mind pushes its way into the moment and questions what it is I am doing, ripping the pleasure away and forcing me to try and shut myself out.

"Tell me about your sexual desires. What have you always wanted a man to do to you?"

I blush at the question, knowing the answer, but I don't want to tell him.

When I remain silent, he tries a different angle. "Why are you embarrassed to tell me?"

"It's a secret," I whisper, as if I don't even want the room to know.

"Why?"

"Because..."

"Because?"

"It just is."

"Mm." He doesn't sound pleased with my answer. "And what is your secret worth?"

I pause at his question. "What do you mean?"

"Who are you trying to keep this secret from?"

I think about it for a few seconds. "Everyone?"

"What's the point in that?"

"What do you mean?" I frown, and my fingers stop their circling, just resting in the wet heat of my pussy as I ponder his words. "It's a secret."

"Of your deepest desires?"

"Yes."

"So if you keep it from everyone, how would they ever get fulfilled?"

"I don't know."

He lets the words hover between us, suspended in an invisible world of copper wires that tether us together. "It must be very dark then."

"I don't know if that's how I'd put it."

"How would you put it then? It must be worth a lot for you to keep it buried so deep inside you. What would it cost for you to reveal it?"

"Cost?"

"If your secret is so deep and dark, so deeply buried, it must be big, but like everything, secrets have worth." He falls into a short silence, "That said, with secrets, we trade differently; their worth is measured only in their grandeur and in the number of people from which we hide them."

I nod at the phone, taking in his logic. Trying to make sense of it.

"I didn't say you could stop touching yourself."

As if by themselves, my fingers begin circling my clit, and a soft moan cascades from my lips.

"Now, are you ready to trade?" He wants to turn my words into things, my thoughts into a business contract, my feelings into an object to trade - and I am about to let him.

"Mmmm," I manage as my fingers bring me closer to

pleasure once again, building up that sensation between my legs that has me needing so much more than a voice on the phone, that have me remembering the neglect of my own body and my crippled soul.

"What is your secret worth?"

"One of yours," I pant out as my orgasm builds.

"A fair trade," he says and then waits for me to spill.

My body heats up as I gather courage to voice out my desires, and my clit throbs as I stroke it harder now. "I've always wanted a man to blindfold me and hold me down while teasing me mercilessly till I beg him to let me come." My eyes are clenched shut picturing my fantasy, and my hand now moves in a wild frenzy. I grind against my fingers seeking pleasure, pleasure I have not felt in forever, the sensation overwhelming, overpowering.

"Sensory deprivation?" There's surprise in his voice and also delight, but it doesn't matter now because I have pushed myself over an edge and I fall. All my muscles tense and tremble, my back arches and a series of hungry desperate whimpers fall from my lips as pleasure explodes across my body. My head whips back into the pillow, and I writhe on the bed, grinding against my own hand, seeking every last inch of pleasure I can give myself.

When the last of the shivers stop, I lay wasted and panting on the bed, a sheen of sweat on my forehead, and I allow myself a minute to dissolve into the sheets, melt away into aa exquisite oblivion.

"Thank you for that, that was beautiful."

Heaving a lungful of air, I blink a few times then shake myself out of my daze. *Fuck.* The voice on the phone. He fell into the void, and for a few blissful moments, I forgot about his existence, about my existence, about everything but the singular sensation between my legs that spread into my body and overwhelmed all my senses. A new sort of heat coats my body; an overriding anxious embarrassment at allowing this total stranger to listen to me. At telling him my deepest desires, at revealing all of myself. He is a stranger to me, but he knows my room number, he could know what I look like, he could know... everything. I start to spiral, my writer mind creating thousands of dark scenarios in an instance, the pleasure washed away by dark fingers of fear and anxiety.

"Relax." His voice pierces my panic. It's kind; he knows.

I suck in a few long breaths, trying to collect my frazzled thoughts, put the pieces together and find a reality in which I am not this pathetic creature I've become.

"I owe you a secret."

His words fill me with courage and hope. "I didn't think..."

"That I'd stick around long enough to let you collect?"

"Well..." I am once again full of shame. But then again, the world is harsh and unforgiving, and I've learned many grim lessons.

"I guess not everyone would."

"No, they wouldn't." We agree and sit in a slow comfortable silence.

"Ask me then." He sounds relaxed, confident, like he doesn't have a worry in the world. Like all his secrets are guarded, but not as heavily as mine.

I twirl my finger through the phone wire, and a thousand questions swirl inside my head, but just as soon as I think of them they fall away; they all seem trivial or unmatched to my own secret. I'm tempted to ask for his name, but that's not a secret, not really, not for the rest of the world outside this room. Or if he's done this sort of thing before, or why he hasn't tried to call the number he was actually dialling. But none of those are secrets and none would reveal his dark heart like I revealed mine. So I go for the simplest question, the most obvious, the easy way out.

"Do you like what I like? Would you let someone blindfold you and tease you and take away your power?"

"That's three questions."

"With a singular answer."

"Touché."

I feel like he might be stalling. "Would you?"

"I would have to trust the person explicitly."

"And is there no one in your life that you do?"

"Maybe one."

"And where is she?"

"She's gone."

"I'm sorry," I say as my heart squeezes in my chest.

"No. Not like that." He reads my tone perfectly. "We're just not together anymore."

"Oh."

"We should have never really been together in the first place." Something changes in his voice then, an undercurrent of melancholy.

"How's that?" I ask, my curiosity getting the better of me.

"She's my ex-wife's best friend."

"I see."

"It wasn't like that."

"I didn't say anything." I defend myself though there should be no reason for me to.

"I was already broken up with my wife, and her best friend was dating this douche who one day just packed up and left—went back home overseas. No explanation, no reasoning—he just left her." He's angry now; the calm demeanour he'd kept till now, rickety and cracking like an old wharf. "We were both a little heartbroken and we were friends. I mean, I've known her for years; she's the godmother of my daughters. She came over for a meal and a chat, and one thing led to another you know…"

I nod. "I do." But I don't. Maybe the better phrasing would be *I understand*. But I've never had that happen to me. I guess I don't keep those kinds of friends. Or any friends.

"The sex was amazing. We had such chemistry, and fuck, she was sexy as hell. But after that first time, we both agreed that it was a mistake, that it shouldn't have happened and that it won't happen again. But then it did, again and again, and then over time, it became so much more. It wasn't just about that physical need we craved from one another; it was companionship. She was incredible—in every fucking way. We would talk about our day, about everything really. Watch TV, steal kisses. And I was so enamoured with her, amazed that someone like her could be with someone like me." He draws in a deep breath, and I feel his pain through the other side of the phone. My heart squeezes in my chest.

"So, what happened? Where is she?"

There's a long silence, and I wonder if I've overstepped when he finally starts speaking again.

"One morning I left for work, kissed her goodbye as I always did, and tucked her into the bed. When I came back, she was gone." His voice cracks and he clears his throat before continuing. "A few hours later she sent me a text. Apparently, the boyfriend came back and she went back to him. No goodbyes, no explanations." His pain spills out of the phone and floods my room. I lift my legs, cradling them into my chest, not wanting to dip my feet in it.

"Did you try to reach out?"

"No."

"Why?" I know I shouldn't be asking, but the longing in his voice reels me in, pulling on my own heartstrings.

"How could I? She's with him, and I have to see her at school events and family things—when I'm invited." He empties his lungs with a shallow sigh. "It doesn't matter—it was three years ago. She bloody married the douche. And we never spoke about it, not once." He sounds so strained, so fragile, and my heart feels strangled.

"You miss her."

"Of course."

"You never got your closure."

"No." His subdued laughter mocks me, and suddenly my secret seems so trivial in the face of his. "The thing is, there's no one I can talk to about it. Not then, not now. She's my ex's best friend; they're like sisters. If my ex ever finds out... she will take my daughters away from her. She doesn't have kids of her own, she would lose everything..."

"And you're not over her." How could he be? He never got his answers. He doesn't get to examine the pieces of the puzzle she's left behind; he can't assemble it or move on. Endings are painful, but he never got an end, just an empty bed and endless silence.

He sighs. "Maybe, maybe not. To be honest, I'm not sure what I miss more, her or our friendship, you know? That companionship, that fills the empty spaces. And sometimes I ask myself if I should have fought harder, chased more, let everyone know."

"But...?"

"But she left. She chose him. I feel like that's a pretty resounding no." The strong commanding man that had me playing with myself moments ago, crumbles on the other end of the phone, his walls collapsing and his vulnerability as sharp and raw as my own. I want to reach for him.

I keep him talking, unburdening. "And since her?"

"There was one more girl. We worked together and we had a thing for about six months, then she left me too, but we shared an office and I couldn't really tell anyone about it either, you know?"

"So you've had no one to talk to about any of this?"

"I guess not." Tears prickle my eyes as I think of him as Sisyphus and the boulder he rolls up the hill for eternity. Such is the weight of his grief and his pain with no one to help him shoulder the burden.

"You have no friends?"

"I do. I mean, I lost some good ones when we split up, as you do—and the ones I have now, they're mostly work colleagues, and I spend most of my days asking how they are. It's part of my job."

"Asking them how they are?"

"Yeah, there's this one guy whose mother is really sick; he's been helping her out. I try to help him where I can. Letting him go early and things like that, and a few other guys are having trouble with their families. Anyway, they're not the kind of people I can talk to about this."

"And who asks you if you're okay?"

"No one." He stops short, as if realising the depth of his loneliness. My body shudders at his pain, as if recognising it as my own. "That's pretty fucking depressing, isn't it?" The strength all but gone from his voice. My heart stutters in my chest and a sadness spills from it, filling me with a familiar iciness.

"I'm asking," I say, hoping to push away some of the cold that's making my fingertips tingle.

"But we're strangers, voices on the end of a line."

"So?"

"So, I think, I am clearly not okay. And this was a mistake." He's silent again, and all I hear is my thumping heart as it keeps aching for him.

"Or maybe it wasn't." I look at myself in the mirror. The dishevelled hair and bare torso, the overhanging tracksuit pants, and black circles under the eyes. Hope can come in many shades. I may not be the brightest light, but even a dim light is worth grasping at.

"Maybe." I can almost feel him shrug on the other end. "I have this house all set up for my girls and I can't even see them."

"What do you mean?"

"My ex, she won't let me have them, well not overnight anyway."

"What do you mean?"

"Just that—she won't let me see them unless she needs something from me."

"Oh."

"I've set up this house for my daughters who I can't see, and I have this bedroom with two bedside tables and two lamps, but it's just me. I have no one to share it with." He chokes on his words.

The silence stretches between us for a long time.

"Hey, I better go," he says, his voice sounding resolute and broken all at once.

"No! Wait." I don't think, but I know deep inside me I can't let him hang up, not yet, not now.

"You know where I am staying, and you know my room number."

"Yes."

"Then come over, now, we can have a drink and watch a movie."

"I... erm... don't..."

"My name is Andi. Please...?"

"Chris."

"Please, Chris, come have a drink with me. Let's be alone together."

He's silent again, only his breathing letting me know he's still on the line. "That's not a good idea."

"Then a movie, we can just sit and watch TV till we fall

asleep." My heart chugs in my chest, and it feels like a freight train is trying to push its way through me.

"Thanks for listening, Andi."

"Will you come?" My eyes dart to the toiletries bag that still sits at the end of the bed. "Please?" And suddenly I don't know which one of us I am trying to save.

"Goodnight, Andi."

The line cuts off and all that's left is silence. But he didn't actually say no, or yes, just goodnight. What the hell does that mean?

I pace furiously as I wait, my heart throbbing in my chest as I am consumed by worry and anxiety, then equal parts excitement, equal parts disappointment for every minute that he doesn't show up. He's given me my own puzzle to examine, a picture that might never become complete. After half an hour, I give up and my hope plummets to the floor like a speck of dust in space. I guess it never really mattered.

I walk towards the bed, resigned, about to crawl under the blanket and force myself to sleep and find a reason to wake up in the morning. But then I hear it. It's faint at first, barely there, but then I hear it again, firmer this time, more certain than before.

I open the door.

"Andi?" I nod, smile and step aside letting him in. He's taller than I thought he would be, but then it's impossible to gauge someone's height by their voice. He smiles back, not a toothy grin, but a shy vulnerable grin that has his lips and the edges of his bright blue eyes tipping up.

"Chris?" He nods and runs a hand across his clean-shaven chin. "It's nice to meet you."

We stand there for a few moments just looking at one another. There's something about the way he looks at me, like for the first time in a long time I'm actually being seen.

"Come in." I close the door behind him and take the few steps to the bed, climb on, and push my pillow against the headboard. The woman from the next room remembers herself and she's moaning again. Chris looks up, amused, and tilts an eyebrow. I shrug, and his mouth splits in a lovely smile. I like his face when he smiles. I like his face.

He toes off his shoes while his eyes sweep over the many tiny empty bottles that stand in a line under the TV. He says nothing. Reaching for the toiletries bag that still lays open on the bed, he collects it and sets it on the rounded dining table before climbing on the bed next to me. Setting up his own pillow and leaning back into it. He stretches himself along the bed and crosses his long legs at the ankles.

"What do you want to watch?" I ask him, grabbing the remote.

"You pick."

I flick through the channels till I come across an 80s action movie. It's a classic. I set the remote down and relax against the pillow. We sit in silence and let the movie play out. I don't know when we edged so close to one another, or when my head rested on his chest and his arm cloaked around me, but I like being alone together with Chris. For the first time in I can't even remember I feel like a real person, not an imaginary one that lives on the pages of made-up stories. I feel like I might want to rejoin the land of the living and really, I don't feel so fucking lonely.

5

ROOM #538 – JESSE'S GIRL

Tylor

Everything is so fucking shiny and glittery, and she is smiling from ear to ear like a fucking Cheshire cat that needs to be kicked in the face and taken down a notch. That fucking girl always smiles, except when she looks at me. I have this incredible quality to erase that smile right off her fucking stupid beautiful face. Anyway, I just don't get what the hell she finds so thrilling all the fucking time. I mean, sure, it's possibly the fact that she is head over heels in love with Rob, and the fact that she's spent the last year organising this trip with me as a surprise for him and we actually managed to pull it off.

This fucking girl, with her tiny little tops and tiny little skirts, just showed up at my house out of the blue and told me she wants to surprise Rob with a trip away on his 21st birthday, and as I'm practically his brother and best mate, I have to come too.

I spent the first half an hour talking to her about stalking people and the fact that she shouldn't be at my house, then spent the next year hating every second I had to spend with her. Hating the way she smelt and giggled when I made a sarcastic remark that should have insulted her. Hating that she always had a smart-ass comment for me, hating the way her shirt always rides up her navel to reveal her flat fucking stomach and the way she runs her fingers over her mouth when she's deep in thought. But most of all, I hate how much she loves Rob and how much effort she's put into this trip, even though I saw her first. Even though I wanted her first, even though she fucking chose *him*. Because why the fuck wouldn't she?

Rob is like a sun god, all bright and blond and bronzed, and me, well, I look like I just walked out of the pits of hell; dark and brooding and abrasive, or so I've been told.

Three months ago, I met Liv. She's pretty enough and likes to think she's super cool—dressed like an emo with her black clothes and her black nails and her black lipstick. She's sweet enough and intelligent enough and sucks a cock like a pro, so I asked her to come with us. What I really needed was a distraction, someone to take my mind off the fact that V isn't mine. And that I'd be sharing a room with her and my best friend and hearing them fuck while I'll be pretending to sleep. The mere thought sends a thrill of green jealousy through me and flares my fucking anger. Or maybe I wanted something to make V jealous, to make her see that she'd lost her opportunity to be with me, but she just kept fucking smiling and telling me how good we look together. That fucking girl...

Liv is hanging off my arm just as excited as V. The two of them get on like a house on fire, and it shits me. This fucking girl could get along with Stalin.

We checked in a couple of hours ago. The room is a twin; two double beds right next to each other with a TV and minibar. V's scent has already seeped into every crevice of the room, and her scent makes my cock rock-hard. Liv gets all excited thinking it's for her. She keeps whispering in my ear to fuck her in the bathroom. I keep pushing her off and offering her another drink. She pouts and makes that disappointed face, but I don't give a shit. I don't want to fuck her. Not yet... maybe later, when I have to fuck all my frustrations out. I'll break her fucking pussy thinking of V, thinking about all the things that make me want to close my hands around her throat and squeeze.

Of course, we have a few drinks in the room. Yeah, we've been saving for a year, but fuck, this place is expensive, and I still have rent and student loans to pay off. I push those thoughts aside just like I push away the thoughts of having V spend the night in Rob's arms right next to me.

Not that she hasn't stayed the night in our apartment before. Not that I haven't heard them, but the thought of him fucking her a metre away from where I sleep is fucking with my brain. The thought of his hands on her ass as she rides his cock has me seeing all kinds of shades of red.

"Let's get a drink," V says, cutting through my thoughts. She's pulling Rob, their hands laced together, and Liv yanks my arm following them to the bar.

At the bar, the girls study the cocktail menus. "No cocktails," I announce, "this is a celebration. We're doing shots."

I wave the barman over and ask him for four shots of tequila.

V glares at me; she's always fucking doing that. "This is a classy place—"

"It's Rob's birthday. We can have a few shots, just get that carrot out of your ass for one night and have some fun."

"Hey, man," Rob starts, but she cuts him off.

"I don't need you defending me against *him*." Then she's right there in my face where I knew she would be. "I don't have a carrot in my ass, and I know just how to relax. It's just that..."

I raise an eyebrow, waiting for her to finish that sentence and show me just how relaxed she is by explaining in detail why we shouldn't be doing this. Instead, the barman arrives with our shots and places them in front of us.

I take mine, challenging V. Without hesitation, she grabs her shot glass, as do Liv and Rob. "Happy birthday, brother." I tip my glass towards him and smirk at V as I down my shot.

I watch her bring the shot glass to her mouth and tip the drink back, then wince as the alcohol burns her mouth. She reaches for the sliced lemon and sucks at it. My cock is hard and throbbing, wanting her mouth around me, sucking hard.

I put my hand up for another round, and V stares at me. "Got something to say, princess?"

She frowns. "Not to you." She moves away from me and into Rob, standing with her back to his chest where he wraps a hand around her waist and places a kiss on her neck. I turn away, waiting for our shots to arrive while Liv tries to grind against me. I turn my body away and lean against the bar, staring at the bottles all lined up like colourful bowling pins.

The shots arrive and we all down them. I keep my gaze averted.

"What do you feel like doing?" V turns to Rob after pulling a decimated lemon wedge from her mouth.

"There's a pool room just around the corner. Let's go there."

"Great, let's go," she says, already leading us away from the bar.

We weave our way through the casino floor; machines and twinkling lights everywhere. When we enter the pool room, the lights are dimmed and the jingling from outside dies down, replaced by background rock music and pool balls smacking each other as they fall away into their holes.

V finds an empty pool table and runs off to the bar. I follow her, leaving Liv and Rob at the table. My body is pushed against her, and my hard cock sweeps against her soft ass as we're crammed by the crowd trying to replenish their drinks.

"She turns to glare at me. "Do you mind?"

"No," I say and ignore her as I try to catch the attention of the barman. She huffs and tries to wiggle away, the sensation making my cock swell even more in my pants, and I let out a harsh breath that's drowned away by the noise around us.

The barman asks what we want. V gets a card for the table with twenty dollars, and I get Rob and Liv another shot, a beer for myself, and a pink cocktail for V. She eyes me as the barman puts the order in front of me. I ignore her and hand her her drink. She murmurs a subdued thank you. Of course, I'm not trying to be chivalrous, but I know she'll sip on the drink nice and slowly.

We return to the others, and V slots the card into the table, releasing the balls. "Let's play doubles," she announces and hands a pool cue to Rob. I take a long sip from my beer and watch V set up the balls in the triangle. She's already bending over the table reaching, and I can't help but stare at her plump ass, the shape of it teasing me, begging me to sink into it.

Liv and I win the first game and the second. Liv is useless, but I'm not about to let Rob win cause it's his birthday. V keeps frowning at me, probably thinking I should make it easy for him, but fuck her, I have no interest in letting her win. I order Liv and Rob another round of shots as I sip on my beer slowly and watch as V's drink has hardly been touched.

"You trying to get me drunk, brother?" Rob slaps my shoulder as he tips his shot glass towards me.

"Only trying to improve your game." I wink at him, and he laughs before downing his shot.

Liv is already halfway gone, hanging off me and giving me sloppy kisses. "You're so hot," she whispers in my ear and pushes up on her tiptoes, her mouth covering mine. I glance up to see V is watching so I kiss her back, opening my mouth to Liv, tasting the alcohol on her breath. As my tongue sinks deeper into her mouth, my eyes stay locked on V until she looks away, then I break the kiss and smirk, my body throbbing. Liv pushes up again. "Fuck me in the bathroom," she says.

I look into her face. She's half drunk and thirsty for my cock; she reaches for it, feeling how hard I am, and her eyes glow. I push her hands away and bend down to whisper in her ear, my eyes catching V's as she glares at us. "Later, baby," I whisper darkly, knowing I have no intentions of fucking her tonight. She gives me a dirty smile before turning away, and I smack her ass for good measure as she walks away. She giggles, and V rolls her eyes. I wink at her, and she looks away and back to Rob, who is already setting up for the next game, a little unstable on his feet. I wave down a waiter and order him another shot.

"I'm going to sit this one out," Rob says and finds a seat; his eyes are already taking on that hazy blur and his words are slightly slurred. V is by his side, tucking herself between his legs as his hands close around her ass.

"Are you okay, baby?" She's studying his face.

"Yeah, I'm great. Why don't you play a game against Tylor? Beat him for me." She whips her head back and stares at me, and I give her my best smirk as I wave at the table.

"I will," she promises and kisses him gently. I tear my eyes away and set them firmly on the balls as I set them up in the triangle.

The break is sloppy. I hit the white too hard and slightly askew. Watching her kiss him flared my irritation. She's trying to play with me, but she's not going to win.

"Nice break," she mocks me as a few balls break away from the centre and the rest remain in a group hug in the middle of the table.

I ignore her and watch her body as it bends over the table, her skirt riding all the way up, showing off the swell of her ass cheeks. I swallow hard, unable to tear my eyes away.

She sinks a couple of balls and gets all excited and bouncy. I grind my jaw as I watch her look to Rob for approval. His smile is there, but it's heavy, as are his limbs.

She misses, and I go to the table for my shot. Bending over I set the yellow ball in my sights before I feel her; she's standing close, her hip kissing mine. "That's an easy shot."

I don't look up at her. "Shut it already. I'm concentrating."

"I'm just saying, it's hard to miss." Her hip slides along mine and her tone is velvety and sweet in a way that taunts me.

I glance up at her then stand, our bodies almost flush. "You don't think I know what you're doing?"

"What am I doing?" She flutters her eyelashes at me and smirks. My jaw ticks at our closeness, and I remain silent staring into her eyes, barely holding myself back from grabbing her, bending her over the table and fucking her hard in front of everyone in this fucking room. Instead, I remind myself she belongs to Rob and take a step back, then readjust the cue in my hand, setting up for the shot.

My hand pulls back as her hip grinds slowly against mine and her voice rings out, "I mean, a kid could probably—"

"Fuck." The cue slips off my fingers and hits the white ball on the wrong side, setting it bouncing in the wrong direction and missing the ball I was aiming for altogether, instead, hitting one of her reds and setting it up for a perfect shot. I stand up, turning towards her. "Look at what you did. Are you fucking happy now?"

She shrugs.

"Feeling pretty good about yourself, huh?"

"It's easy to get in your head, Tylor." She winks at me, her voice low and seductive. My gaze flicks over to Rob, who is busy laughing at the scene.

"Oh yeah? Well, what am I thinking right now?"

"Uhm... about how you're going to get your ass handed to you by me and never live it down." She giggles. Fucking giggles and grabs her cue before lining up her shot and sinking yet another ball.

I suck in a long deep breath through my nose and let it out as I watch her lithe body bend over the table. She looks over her shoulder and gives me a quick look before sinking another ball in its pocket. I sink my teeth into my lower lip and bite down hard, then find a waiter and order Liv and Rob two more shots and another beer for me. V can go fuck herself.

When the drinks come, she pouts. "Nothing for me?"

"Your boyfriend can buy you a drink." I don't even try to hide the bitterness in my voice. The lines in her forehead deepen and she huffs, walking towards him and wrapping herself in him.

Liv is a sloppy mess and keeps trying to touch me. I'm so sick of her advances and her hands on me. When we get back from this trip, I'm going to send her packing. She's served her purpose. I muse about leaving, getting as far away from V as possible, leaving her to Rob and his promising career and promising future. The two of them look like they were made for each other. Two perfect fucking specimens. It's probably why I want to ruin them so badly.

I take another shot and miss. My mind is no longer on the game. V comes up and sinks her final two balls, then the black in quick succession. She yelps and does a little victory dance that has her hips swinging and my cock aching. She runs to Rob, who takes her in his arms and whispers something in her ear, making her giggle. Liv tries to comfort me for losing, and I clench my hand hard around my pool cue and push away from her, taking another long sip from my beer.

Rob challenges me to another game. He's unsteady on his feet and his speech is slurred. He's wasted, just as every twenty-one-year-old should be on their birthday. I annihilate him and feed him two more shots.

We play a few more games, but Rob and Liv have gone well beyond the point of happy drunk and have crossed the line to paralytic, barely standing, barely talking, barely really there. The security guards approach us and ask us to remove ourselves. I nod and reach for Rob, sliding his arm over my shoulder.

I drag Rob through the lobby, and he leans on me with his entire weight; his eyes are droopy and his legs keep buckling. I know I should have stopped feeding him alcohol long ago, but fuck, you only turn twenty-one once, might as well drink enough to forget it.

Liv is just as useless and is hugging V like they've been lifelong friends. She's crying and laughing and giggling like mad, and every now and then, she goes deathly silent and trips over her own feet before bursting into another babble of laughter.

V keeps holding onto her, and when the lift pings, I drag Rob inside followed by V with Liv. We look like a deranged mismatched couple, but no one gives us a second glance.

Must be pretty standard around here.

A beautiful couple that's been patiently waiting for the elevator steps inside in front of us. She's in a long blue dress and he's in a suit that seems tailored to his body. They look perfect, and I'm sick of them already. They make the small space feel crowded, or maybe that's Rob leaning on me and Liv trying to grab onto my cock every few seconds.

On the third floor, the elevator stops, and a man walks inside. He's tall and dark and is wearing jeans and a T-shirt. He barely glances in our direction before he presses level 22.

When we reach our floor, we step out, leaving them all behind.

We enter the room and I slot the card into the electric box. The room explodes in lights that are way too bright. I set Rob onto the bed, and he remains there, listless. Completely paralytic.

"What have you done to him?" V is staring at me as Liv prances like a deranged fairy around the room.

"Me? He's a big boy, he chose to drink."

"You were the one who kept feeding it to him."

"It's his birthday and I'm his best friend, and if I remember correctly, you were the one who insisted I be here, insisted I make sure he has a 'good time'."

"Not like this!" As she hurls the words at me, we hear the gurgling from the bathroom followed by the sickening noise of Liv emptying her guts into the toilet. Lovely.

A few moments later she flushes and the water runs. V is still staring at me like I am somehow responsible for all of this, for all of them. The thing is she is right, I am responsible for this, and I have no issues at all with what's happening around me just now.

Liv stumbles out of the bathroom. Her face is pale and a sheen of either cold sweat or cold water covers her face. "I don't feel so good," she says as she makes her way to the bed, grabbing a pillow. She makes her way back to the bathroom and closes the door behind her.

"Fucking perfect!" V says as she takes a look around the room; her boyfriend passed out on the bed and the closed door with a sleeping pixie on the floor on the other side.

"Stop blaming me for all of this!" I can't help but let my eyes rake all over her, her short fucking skirt and tiny little top with her beautiful, perky breasts showing just the perfect amount of cleavage. She sure knows how to play with a guy's imagination.

"It is your fault! All of this!" She's closer to me now and a finger is pointing at my chest.

"Don't you fucking point at me!" I say, and instead of dropping her finger, she pokes me with it, hard, in the chest.

"Don't!" I growl at her, irritation and desire blending inside me.

"You! You're a total fucking mistake, you ruin everything you touch. I should have never invited you."

"Get your finger out of my face. Final warning, V."

"Or else what? What else could you possibly do to make this weekend any worse?"

I don't think, I just react, and reach for her, sinking my hands into her hair and tugging, hard, then smashing my mouth against hers. The kiss is hot and hard and even when she pretends to fight it, her mouth opens up to me, and I feel how quickly she loses herself to me, how her rigid body folds around me, her hands digging into my back, my shoulders, my hair, till a second later she comes to her senses and pushes me away.

"What the fuck are you doing?" Her eyes dart to Rob who is still passed out on the bed, his breaths shallow.

"What you've been wanting me to do to you for months," I say as I grab her wrist and throw her onto the bed.

"Tylor, don't," she says in a weak voice. She's confused,

but it's okay, I'm about to bring her total clarity. This girl that I've wanted in my bed for a fucking year. That kiss was just a prelude, a delicious fucking introduction to the feast of V, and I intend to indulge fully.

"Why?" I fall to my knees at the end of the bed and pull V's body towards me, even as I do I can smell her arousal. She can say whatever she wants, her body can't lie.

"Cause,… Rob." She's already panting, and her eyes shoot back to the body less than a metre away from us. My best fucking friend, the man who is like a brother to me, who has had my back so many times I've lost count and whose girlfriend I've been in love with for the past year and a half.

"Then tell me to stop," I say as I pull her ever closer to me and spread her legs apart. Her skirt hitches up, and I kiss the delicate soft flesh of her inner thigh. She gasps at the kiss, but she's yet to say anything, so I kiss her again, and again, making my way towards her pussy, the prize; the main meal. I'm so fucking eager to taste her, I'm fucking salivating and the smell alone has me delirious. I've always known she'd smell fucking delicious, taste fucking delicious, but she has my head turned upside down and my cock as hard as fucking rock, and I've barely even touched her.

I nuzzle my nose into her panties and inhale her. She's fucking intoxicating. No amount of drugs or alcohol could ever get me higher than the smell of this girl's pussy. I've barely had a taste and I'm already an addict. I bite down softly over the fabric, and she moans, the sound shooting straight to my cock. Skimming my lips over her cotton-covered pussy, I smirk as I find her underwear soaking wet. Little miss V is a big fat liar.

She moans again, and my cock swells in my pants. "Tell me to stop." This time I'm begging her to, because once I sink my fingers into her pussy, flick my tongue over her sweet little clit and taste her, I won't stop. I simply won't be able to control myself anymore.

"Tylor," my name cascades from her lips, and all I hear is a plea, but she didn't say stop, so I interpret it in the only way I can.

I kiss her other thigh before I slip two fingers beyond the fabric of her underwear and let my knuckles slide between her lips, and fuck me dead this girl is soaked and ready. I don't know if I've ever been so turned on.

I don't wait any more. I don't know when I'll ever get a chance to do this again, I push her underwear to the side with my fingers and have my first taste of her. I groan as my tongue takes its first taste. V is fucking delicious, just as I knew she would be. Salty and musky and whatever girls that turn on boys like me are made of.

She gasps and whispers my name, and I almost come in my pants, but the whisper isn't lustful, it's full of fear and trepidation. Rob is RIGHT THERE, Liv is just behind that door, what we are doing is wrong, but I can't fucking stop, not now that I've tasted her. So I don't. Instead, my tongue explores her beautiful pussy, slowly and meticulously. I run it up and down and taste all her fucking flavours, flicking over her clit, swirling my tongue around it. She moans for me; a soft delicate sound that she bites away as her eyes keep flicking from my face to his. It only urges me on. A part of me wants him to wake up to see my face buried between her legs, taking what's his, and yet I know it would break them.

Still, I don't stop, inserting two fingers into her as I start to work her more, sliding my fingers in and out as my tongue slides over her clit, teasing sucking swirling, till her breaths become ragged and her legs start to shake. My free hand slides up her belly; it's delicate and soft like the rest of her, and I push my hand hard, forcing her bra over her breasts, desperate for a nipple. I almost come in my pants as I find it. I want to see what it looks like, I want to see the colour of it and know what it feels like to drag my teeth over it, and I know I will allow myself time to find out. I pinch her nipple as my tongue and fingers keep working her. She arches into me, her hips rolling against my face, fucking it, speeding up, grinding against me, giving me all of her.

She's moaning, soft barely-there moans that she bites under her tight bottom lip, one hand clutching the bed sheet, the other pulling at my hair, tugging the strands, pushing me into her, demanding more. Her back bows and her legs lock around me, and she breaks under the pleasure, grinding into me, biting down her scream. Locking her thighs so tightly around my head, for a moment there is no air or escape, just all the shades of V as she explodes into my mouth, and I can't help but delight in all of her. Wanting more, wanting so much more. I keep licking, lapping and kissing till slowly the anaconda around my neck loosens, and the hand in my hair releases the strands, and V sinks into the bed, lying in a puddle of pleasure.

She looks like a wrecked goddess, all flushed and sweaty, with her just-fucked hair and her skirt running up her hips, her underwear pushed to one side and her shirt pushed roughly over her fucking perfect tits, but I'm not done breaking her, not by a long shot.

I don't give her time to recover, to regret, to think. I pull my cock out, inching my jeans down, baring my ass and then I am inside her in one quick shove. I don't know what's sweeter; the feel of her warm pussy clenching around me, or the sweet little moan that trickles from her lips as I sink all the way in. To the hilt.

Her eyes fly open at the intrusion and lock on my face. I still inside her, feeling her warmth and clenching walls that close around me, accommodating, inviting. I wait. I wait for her to tell me to stop, to scream at me and shove my body away, to look longingly at Rob who snores beside us. But she doesn't, she just keeps staring into my eyes, frozen.

"Tylor." My name is a moan, a plea, a curse. "We shouldn't be doing this." Her eyes dart to the man she loves.

"Then tell me to stop." All she has to do is tell me she doesn't want me, this, and I'll pull up my pants and go jerk off in the bathroom with all her juices still on my cock. Even if I don't get to come inside her, I can live off the memory of her taste and the feel of her pussy around my cock. It can feed me for years.

She remains silent, like I knew she would. I pull out, till just my tip is inside her, then slam back inside her, eliciting a gasp from her beautiful fucking lips. And then I kiss her. I kiss her so fucking hard, pouring all my hate into that kiss. All the months that I've had to endure watching them together, all the misery and hunger I felt, I give it all to her and she takes it and begs me for more. Her hips try to force my rhythm. She wants me, but she wants me quickly; she's still afraid Rob will wake up. He can see how I'm fucking his girlfriend, destroying our friendship, ruining so many beautiful things, but the truth is, I want to prolong this as long as I can. I want her to know how much I hate her. I hate that I was never enough for her. I hate that I made her my enemy, and made my fucking heart a casualty, but most of all, I hate how much I fucking need her, how much I fucking want her, and how I know that even after tonight—this—she will never be mine.

I pull out again, just to the tip, and slide back inside her, while my lips find her fucking nipple and I get to finally wrap my tongue around it, feeling it harden in my mouth as her pussy coats my cock with more of her wetness. She's arching into me now. She wants so much more from me, and I want to give her everything she needs, but first I'm going to take everything I want.

With a swift move, I pull out of her, push off my knees and roll myself onto the bed leaving her on the edge. She turns to look at me. If she wants my cock, she will have to take it. I want to know that she wants this, but more importantly, I want her to know. She rolls onto her stomach and crawls over to me, her mouth closes on mine, and she tells me just how much she hates me too. She hates that she wants me, but she won't stop. Her teeth tug at my lower lip, our tongues battle and swirl. Her hands jerk to my shoulders and creep up my neck, plunging into my hair.

She breaks our kiss to pull the shirt from my body and does the same to her own. Her beautiful perky tits gently glide against my chest with each rise and fall of her body, and hungry desire courses through my veins. A cruel savage thrill slithers through me as she confirms what I've felt, what I've known all this time. I pull away, unable to hold back my smirk, my triumph, my salvation.

"I hate you," her warm breath whispers over my mouth, and her eyes burn with dark intensity.

"I hate you too." Her tongue is back in my mouth—an angry, frantic kiss.

My hard cock jerks between us, and she tears aside her underwear. Her warm pussy glides against me, so wet and hot. My cock twitches and strains, and I groan like a desperate man wanting to be inside her again, to have any part of her, to make her mine.

"Fuck," I groan against her hot skin and flick out my tongue to taste her, but she's already out of reach.

My hungry eyes burn a trail up her intoxicating torso, and everything inside me tightens watching her body move above mine. I bite down another desperate sound, staring at her hard nipples as her breasts move up and down along with her body.

Her index finger lands on my mouth, silencing me as her eyes dart to Rob. He's barely moved; his even breaths calm, as ours grow more desperate. She withdraws her finger, leaving a long trail from my lips down to my neck and along my torso, making her way to my cock, ever so slowly. I lick my lips in her wake. An amused smile tugs at her lips as if she knows she is breaking me inch by inch, tormenting me with desire.

She grips my cock, squeezes a little, and I know she's about to sink onto it. Every nerve ending screams at me as I fight against all my primal desires not to flip her onto her knees and fuck her senseless like an animal. But then I'd lose, then she could still blame it all on me. Then she would lie to herself.

She hovers just above my cock. Frozen. Waiting for me to become unhinged. Her heat sending me into a maddening desperate spiral. Or maybe she's still fighting some internal battle, maybe she still wants to believe her own lies.

I exhale a desperate breath, my fingers digging into her hips. Not urging, not pushing, just reminding her how much she wants this, how much she wants *me.*

V waits a few more seconds, then ever so slowly lowers herself onto me, letting out a sweet, decadent sound that I will play on repeat in my head forever.

Watching her move above me is like watching a perfect lightning storm—it's fucking beautiful, electric, ruthless. V is a phenomenon. Her thighs slap against mine as she rises and falls; her breasts ripple with her movements. When I slide my thumb over her clit, her mouth falls into a perfect little O and her eyes squeeze shut, and fuck I want to freeze her like this forever with her hair loose and cascading across her shoulders, with her skirt hitched up over her hips, with her sharp pants and the keening sounds she's making for me.

V isn't slow anymore. My hips jerk up to meet her battering pace, bringing us both closer, and my greedy fingers glide up her stomach to roll over her nipples. She moans, losing herself to the pleasure she's chasing. She's loud, loud enough to wake them, loud enough to let me know she's chosen me, and those sounds she makes feed my pleasure, my desire, my hunger for her.

"Tylor," she whimpers my name, and I know it's not desire, it's lust. It's the inevitable wave of pleasure that I feel is gripping her tightly as her pussy squeezes around my cock.

Her head snaps back and she cries out while quivering above me. Her hands clutch my thighs, and she grinds me into her with a jarring pulsing climax. Her tight pussy clenches around me, and I explode with a shattering orgasm, convulsing violently beneath her as she drags me deeper still.

I lie breathless and watch V. A sheen of sweat covers her bare body, and as she settles, she levels me with a look before her face begins to crumble.

I see her hand come, and I let her. Her palm connects with my cheek, leaving behind a hot sting. Without a word, she climbs off me and walks to the bathroom. I watch as her thighs glisten with her juices and my cum as it runs from her. A sickening warmth fills my chest. She stands at the door knowing Liv is there and takes a long breath before she turns the knob and steps inside, shutting the door behind her.

6

———————

IN THE MORNING

Bella

The door closes behind me and a shudder ripples through my body at the finality of it all. My eyes burn from lack of sleep but not much more than the rest of my body. It's still on fire; everywhere Ethan touched is now tainted and raw, like I'm in a new skin, I've shed Isi in that room, and I'm not sure if she will ever come back.

I make my way to the elevator, aware of the fact I'm wearing last night's dress. It's known as the walk of shame, but after last night with Ethan, I don't feel that. I feel fucking liberated, uninhibited, free.

I walk towards the elevator and press the button. My thighs squeeze together as I try to soothe my aching pussy. Ethan kept his promise, using my pussy over and over and over again, with his fingers, his cock, the collection of toys he shoved inside me, and then in the morning—not thirty minutes ago, he kissed it better till I screamed his name and begged him to stop. Of course, he didn't.

Before I left, he asked me why I came upstairs with him and allowed him to use me like his pretty little fuck toy when I wasn't with the agency. I told him that even though I looked beautiful I felt broken and somehow, he'd put me back together again. He gave me his number and told me he'd like to fuck my tight little pussy again, soon, and that he would like to break me some more. I can't help the smile and the thrill of warmth that spreads through me every time I think about it. I clutch the card with his phone number tighter to my chest, and the elevator pings, pulling me out of my thoughts.

I step inside and lose myself in memories when the elevator stops and a man steps inside. There's a moment of odd recognition, like, déjà vu, except this hasn't happened before; it's just that I'm trying to place him. And then I do.

"Good morning, Isi." He gives me a brash smile as his eyes track down my body, clearly taking in my dishevelled hair and makeup, and the fact I am wearing last night's outfit.

"Dean." I smile back at him and notice all the little details that tell me he's had just as busy a night as I had. The red sunken eyes, the days' worth of growth on his face, the hair swept back after a shower, and the same outfit he wore last night that somehow doesn't sit as well as it did the night before.

Our eyes drop away for just a second as we both absorb each other's not so secret secrets.

"Good night?" he asks, and I feel the flush of heat spreading from my chest to my neck along my cheeks and stinging the tips of my ears.

"Yeah, you?"

"Yeah." We both smile that knowing smile, thinking about our respective nights. "I could use a coffee." He winks at me as my smile spreads across my cheeks.

"Coffee sounds good."

He smiles, and we take the rest of the elevator trip in

silence. When the doors swing open, he waves for me to get out first, and I do. He steps out behind me. "The dining room is this way."

I follow him through the corridor and bypass the casino on our left. Not much seems to have changed from last night. The lights are still on and the ringing still blares as people with glassy eyes sit by machines and pull levers and press buttons. I feel different though. The woman that walked into this place less than twenty-four hours ago is gone, somehow twisted and moulded into a new version. A bolder version.

The dining room is busy, and the smell of crispy bacon and freshly baked bread fills the room. My stomach growls and suddenly I'm famished. A woman that could be in her late 40s approaches us. Her hair is slicked back in a tight bun and her white and grey uniform is pristine.

"Two?"

"Yes," Dean answers for us as she looks us up and down, no doubt knowing, no doubt judging. Fuck her and her judgements.

She sits us at a table in the centre of the room. To our left sits a couple. They look cosy as they speak and laugh and whisper at one another over two full plates of food, and to our right is a table with four young kids. They couldn't be much older than twenty. Two of them looks in a bad way, while the other two glare at each other from across the table. They look familiar, like maybe our paths have crossed before, and I think about our elevator ride from the last night.

"Coffee?" Dean interrupts my observations.

"Yeah, that will be great, thanks."

"Are you going to spill that on me too?"

"That depends, are you going to bring me tea instead of coffee?"

"Nah, that stuff will kill you," He chuckles and shakes his head. "And anyway, I usually do my poisoning behind closed doors." He winks as I giggle at him and watch him walk away towards the drinks area.

<hr>

Tylor

I wake up to an empty bed and an emptier feeling. She never came back to me. She left that bathroom with Liv still passed out on a pillow on the floor, then wrapped herself in Rob, even though she smelt like me and was coated in my cum.

I hear them whispering in the bed next to mine, and my fucking stomach churns like it wants to be sick. Like I was the one drinking excessively the night before. I hear her giggle and the sounds of lips meeting skin, and fuck I want to kill someone. But I'm not surprised. Last night was never going to change anything. I try to work out what it was about, as I have been all night. Unable to sleep, craving more of her, willing her to come to me and not to him.

I know she'll tell him. Not today and maybe not tomorrow, but soon this will all blow up in my face, and I'll lose them both. I lick my lips, finding a shade of flavour from last night; remnants of V on my lips, and I suck in a long breath. Fucking worth it.

I hear her groan and push Rob away. "Your breath stinks."

She rolls away from him and leaves the bed. Her eyes land on mine; they are dark and angry. I've ruined her, and I don't care, cause if I get given the chance, I'll ruin her all over again.

Rob rolls onto his back and his eyes land on me a second

before he brings his hands to his face and rubs his eyes as if they are bleeding, then moans. "Fuck, my head hurts."

I laugh at him. "That's cause you drink like a girl."

"Oi." V takes a pillow and throws it at me. I catch it and take a whiff. It smells like her, and my cock comes to life in my pants, reliving every moment of last night in slow motion.

"Fuck you. How do you look so fucking pretty this morning?" Rob groans at me.

"Cause I can handle my booze." I smirk at him. What he doesn't remember won't hurt him. Yet…

"I need a shower," he says and rolls off the bed, swaying. "Want to come help me clean up?" He looks at V and winks, and my entire body tightens. Her eyes dart to me for a second. "I would, but Liv is in there, and she might need a bit of help."

"Let pretty boy over here help her, you're coming with me." He stumbles a little as he ropes his hands around her and picks her up. She squeals in his arms as he marches them into the bathroom. A few minutes later a grey-looking Liv stumbles out. She gives me a weak, embarrassed smile before curling up to me and closing her eyes. She smells like a fucking brewery, and with each inhale the alcohol burns away any remnants of V.

I push up from under her and go stand by the large floor-to-ceiling windows, pulling them open and watching the world beneath my feet. People milling around like ants, cars driving around, the fucking world keeps spinning like it's not a fucking crushing bleak universe where she isn't mine.

The shower door stays closed for far too long, and I loathe the thought of him washing me off her. When they step back into the room, they're both wet and wrapped in towels, and Rob's smile lets me know he feels much better. V is stoic. Her eyes dart to mine fleetingly, and I wonder if she feels the stab of pain I do. She probably thinks it's guilt. Really, it's longing. Maybe one day she'll understand the difference. I march to the bathroom and slam the door behind me. I can't watch. I don't want to.

I wipe away the steam that fogs the mirror and stare at myself, hating everything I see. Fuck. I don't know how long I stand there but eventually, Liv is banging on the door needing the toilet.

I splash some water over my face, open the door, let her in then step out leaving her behind.

"I need food," Rob informs the room in general as V packs away her things and he slaps her ass. I fight the urge to punch him.

I grunt at him and look away.

The shower is on again and on my left, I hear Rob whispering— not so quietly to V— how he wished they had a separate room so that they didn't have to get dressed and could continue what they were doing in the shower. Nausea creeps inside me again, and I keep my gaze firmly fixed on the window, staring at nothing in particular.

"Rob," V whispers harshly, half moaning, and when I look at her, she's under him, and he's trying to fuck her through her clothes. When our eyes meet, she pushes him away and rolls off the bed continuing to pack. He rolls onto his back and laughs, then winks at me when he catches my eye.

I give him a knowing smile and a shrug, the universal—I feel you, bro—then find my shoes.

When Liv finally gets out of the shower, we head out to the dining room. And I'm famished, but the idea of food nauseates me. The idea of eating anything other than V infuriates me.

The three of them come back with their plates piled with food.

"Why so glum?" Rob stares at me as he digs into a pile of greasy bacon and over-easy eggs that trickle through his bread and onto his fingers and plate. He doesn't care as he takes a big bite.

"I'm fine, brother, just wondering how you manage to look so fucking good after all that alcohol you poured into yourself last night, and I still look like I've been run over by a truck."

He chuckles with his mouth full, pieces of egg fly out of his mouth. "That's all V and her magic little body."

"Rob." She swats him and glares at his face. He's not wrong, her body is magic, but I know full well he means her pussy. And my cock tightens in my pants thinking about being inside her.

"You're a lucky man, while poor Liv over here is stuck with the likes of me. Maybe V can give her some tips later on. She can tell her how to score a guy like you." I wink, and he laughs.

"Aww, you're gorgeous, baby," Liv says, but no one is really listening.

"Dumb fucking luck," Rob speaks over her, setting his overloaded bread down and sipping on his coffee.

"Maybe, but you know, I hear that romance and mystery go hand in hand."

"Mystery?" Liv perks up as my eyes settle on V.

"Yeah, you have to be mysterious, hold on to a few secrets."

"Are you keeping secrets from me?" Liv's head tilts to the side and her fork freezes mid-air.

I wrap my hand around her shoulder and get in real close, a smile plastered on my face. "Baby, I have millions of secrets." I wink, and she pushes me away, smiling before taking that bite. I lean back into my chair and focus my attention back on V.

"What about V over here, does she have any secrets?" I ask.

Rob takes another sip and smiles at me. "How would I know? It's a secret, right?" He's amused. V bursts into a nervous giggle next to him and fidgets with her breakfast.

"You know what the best part is about being with a real man? You don't have any reason to lie to him." She leans into Rob and kisses his cheek, her eyes locked on mine.

"Hear that, bro? She called me a real man."

"Pfft, you're no man, I've seen how you drink."

"Yeah, yeah, get fucked."

"I did." I wink at him, and he bursts out laughing looking at Liv who is looking at me and suddenly all eyes on the table are on me, but I only see V, wide-eyed and looking like a rabbit caught in a snare. "It's why I need another coffee." I smirk and get up, leaving the tension behind as Rob groans and Liv rolls her eyes.

I pour myself another coffee and V shows up. She's vibrating with anger. "You need to stop," she says as she snatches an empty cup from the pile.

"What are you talking about?" I feign innocence.

"That little fucking game you're playing."

"So you're not having fun anymore? Cause last night when you were riding my cock..."

"Tylor!" she snaps and looks around us as if everyone can hear. "Just stop it, the game is over."

"Maybe it's not a game."

She glares at me for a long moment. "It's not? Then why not just fucking get it over with and tell him?"

"I don't think now is a good time."

"No? Really? Will it not give you a fucking thrill to

humiliate me? To break us up, to ruin your friendship and this weekend more than you already have?"

"Why the hell would I want to do that?"

Her forehead pulls into an agitated frown. "Why? Probably so you could keep this hanging over my head, so I never know when it's coming, so you can use it against me next time you want to—"

"No," I say, all the jest gone. "And last night, that was just as much you as it was me, so don't lie to yourself, V. We both know the truth."

Her eyes fall away and some of her anger drains from her face "Then what *do* you want, Tylor?"

I wait for her to look at me, to fucking see me like she saw me last night. When her eyes capture mine, they are glistening with unshed tears, and I swallow all the bullshit I was going to spew her way. "You know what I want, V? What I've always fucking wanted, what I wanted from the fucking second I laid eyes on you. You, V. I want you, but you chose him." I turn away with my coffee and go back to the table, leaving her there with my heart in her hands.

As I take my seat, I notice the woman in the blue dress. I remember sharing an elevator with her last night, but I'm pretty sure she was with a different guy. I shrug, I totally know the feeling.

Andi

I wake, and for a second I don't know if I am still dreaming. Heavy hands close around me and I feel his chest moving against my back. It takes me a few seconds to realise that I am in fact awake and that Chris is still in the bed with me. I don't move. I don't want to wake him and I'm enjoying his heat, the feel of him wrapped around me, his heartbeat thudding against my back like a relaxing metronome. I don't know exactly when we fell asleep, but it all felt so natural, so easy. Lovely really.

A moment later I feel him stiffen around me, and I know he's awake, coming slowly to the same realisation I did. It takes a few beats before he relaxes against me and pulls me to him, closer, then kisses the top of my head. We don't speak, just lie there for a while with our own thoughts, feeling another human presence, maybe feeling real, like we are part of this world that's left us behind.

He gets up first and goes to the bathroom. For some reason, I don't dare move. When he steps back into the room, he seems almost sheepish. Not knowing where to go. A stark contrast to the voice that had me coming on my fingers the night before.

I want to thank him for coming and for sleeping next to me, for holding me, for giving me a glimmer of hope, but my cell phone rings, and when I reach for it, it feels like the moment is lost.

I swipe, seeing my agent's name flash on the screen. "Good morning, Agatha." I am once again paying more attention to voices on the phone than actual real people.

"Good morning, Andi." She sounds way too happy for someone who took a chance on a failed writer like me.

I watch Chris give me a half-wave before he turns towards the door. "Wait," I call out to him, "please?"

It feels like there are so many more things for us to say to one another and ending like this in a pregnant silence feels like a cliff-hanger, one I'll never be able to write the ending to by myself. He looks up at me with his piercing blue eyes and stops mid-motion, tilting his head in a slight nod. I sigh in relief.

"How are you?" I can hear the hint of concern in her voice.

"I'm fine," I say to her as I stay locked in a suspended look with Chris. I search his rounded face, his bald head and the growth of hair on his chin and realise I'm not lying.

"Good, good, are you sitting down?"

Still tucked in the bed, I assure her I am. "Andi, take a deep breath."

My heart plummets. I know she is about to tell me the publisher is going to drop me and the career I have chased all my life is over. "So, this book of yours, it's opened up in the top 100 in the book charts. The way that the books are selling, we are projecting that it will be one of the top sellers of this week, and likely to need a reprint by the end of the month."

I sit there in stunned silence, my mouth hanging open. Chris frowns as he looks at me questioningly. I hear the words that she is saying, but I am saturated in disbelief given last night's room full of ghosts.

"Now, I know you were disappointed about last night, we all were, but turns out the paper put out the wrong date in its print, they've put the launch date as tonight. Now, I've already tentatively rebooked the room and spoken to the caterers, but would you consider staying another day and giving the launch another go? I have no doubt everything will look totally different today."

I look at the man standing in the middle of my room. Today already looks very different.

"Okay," I manage to breathe into the phone, and she goes on blathering about how wonderful it will be and how happy she is for me. A moment later there's a knock at the door.

Chris looks at me, and I shrug. He walks over and flings the door open. A bell boy stands on the other end and hands Chris a huge bouquet of flowers and a bottle of champagne. "Congratulations, Andi," he tells him as he hands him the items.

"Thanks," he mumbles as he accepts my gifts and bites down a smile.

Agatha is saying something about texting me the details about today, but I stopped listening a while back. Setting my phone down, I watch Chris approach the bed. He hands me the flowers and the bottle. "I believe these are yours."

"Thank you." I feel heat crawling along my neck and spreading across my cheeks.

"What did you do to deserve that?"

"Nothing special." I shrug and suddenly he is close to me, his eyes dark and his face stark.

"What you did for me last night, Andi, that was special."

The heat intensifies on my face, and my eyes fall away from him, but his knuckles swipe my chin, coaxing my head up till our eyes are level once again. "Not that... well that too, listening to you come...mmm." His groan is deep and guttural, and his eyes close for just a second as he bites down on his bottom lip, and I think my underwear wants to spontaneously combust. "That was beautiful, but you, listening to me, inviting me here, that—that was fucking special."

He holds me there, caught in his gaze for a few more beats, as my heart threatens to batter its way out of my chest, before releasing my chin and leaning back and away from me, giving me a moment to catch my breath.

"I... um... I'm sure plenty of—"

"Don't do that. Don't cheapen what you did by saying everyone else would have. They wouldn't have. They would have let me hang up and left me to sit with my own despair."

He seems so vulnerable, almost at breaking point, and my fingers itch to reach for him, my hands to close around him and blanket his much larger form. To tell him that I don't know how, but I feel like just maybe, possibly, eventually, everything will be alright. But I don't. I just sit there and watch him till he sucks in a long breath and runs a hand over his face before standing up.

"Will you come have breakfast with me?" It's like I want to keep stalling, to keep him near me; prolong whatever *this* is, and I don't know for whose sake; mine or his.

"Sure, breakfast sounds great." His face splits into a half-smile, but it's genuine and sweet and forces some of the pain back.

"I just have to shower." I point at the door, feeling like an idiot, and his grin widens.

"Sure, Andi, go do that."

He waits for me to get off the bed before he climbs back on and switches the TV on. I look at him tentatively, like I'm uncertain about leaving the room.

"I'm not going anywhere," he reassures me as if reading my mind, and I go have my shower.

I step out already dressed and ready to eat and find him still on the bed watching the news. The knots that gathered in my stomach when I was showering, unravelling. "Do you want to stop by your room and shower too?"

He looks at me for a moment, taking me in in my clean summer dress and face made up in natural tones, my hair slicked back after the shower. I look different now that I am not in my oversized shirt and tracksuit pants, and he takes notice. But I feel different also. Like an older version of Andi went to sleep last night, a broken one, a loser, and this morning she woke up brand new with a smidgen of hope and a suddenly potentially thriving career.

"No, I don't have a room at this hotel."

"Oh." Before I have any more time to ask the burning questions, he stands up.

"Let's go."

He ushers us to the elevators, and we stop at the lobby. Chris takes the lead, and I follow to the dining room where the sweet smell of baked goods and fresh coffee slithers through the air and lovingly wraps itself around me.

We find an empty table, and when we sit his knees brush mine. He doesn't try to move them away, instead, he studies my face long and hard before smiling at me. "You are very beautiful, Andi."

He says it like it's the most natural thing in the world, and I look down at my empty cup. "Let's get a coffee."

"Stop doing that."

"Doing what?"

"Not accepting my compliments."

"I just..." I shrug, not wanting to do this right now.

"Just what?"

I sigh, realising he won't let this go, and that maybe because he shared all his secrets with me last night, he feels like I might owe him one more.

"I just don't feel comfortable when people give me compliments."

"Why?" I look away and feel his fingers at my chin again. He forces me to look at his eyes and repeats the question. "Why?"

"I just don't feel like I deserve them really." A silence stretches between us as he studies my face, and tears form in my eyes.

"I understand that completely," he finally says, taking me completely by surprise, then releasing me. "Now let's get that coffee."

We get coffee and fill our plates with food, and while we eat, he tells me about his daughters, sounding like a devoted doting father who only gets glimpses into his children's lives. He tells me about his work and keeps asking about mine. He listens when I tell him about my failed marriage, about the miscarriages and heartbreak, about finding out my ex-husband is going to have a baby with his new girl-friend of only three months. He takes an interest when I tell him about the book I wrote; the one about an invisible man trying to be seen in a world where everyone blends into the background. He makes me laugh, more than once, and his hand swipes over mine a time or two. His knees touch mine the entire time we eat.

When we are nearly done with our breakfast, a beautiful couple walks into the dining room. He is tall and lean and handsome, and she seems overdressed in a beautiful blue flowing gown. They look perfect together. Yesterday I might have resented them. I would have wished to be just like her. She is the kind of person that when she walks into a room everyone notices. The kind of person who is always surrounded by people, while I've always been the kind to feel alone in every room. I used to think people like her never got lonely—and maybe there was a time I would have given anything to be like her, to be noticed, to be the centre of everyone's attention—I wanted a place among people. But I realise that when people like her go home and peel off their beautiful dresses and wash away their fake smiles, they're just as lonely as I am. And this morning, today, right now, I am the centre of attention of one man. Of one single person who sees me and seems to want to keep doing so. So, she can keep her blue dress and long hair and perfect teeth, and I will be me; average and someone's whole world, even for a short moment.

"Would you like anything else?" Chris drags my atten-tion back to him, his eyes focused on my face.

"No, I'm fine."

He nods, and we sit in a comfortable silence, an intimate silence. I reach for his hand, and he doesn't flinch away. His gaze swings from my face to our hands and back to my face. "Can I ask you something?" I ask, stewing in my bravery.

"Okay."

It's not the answer I was hoping for—not a firm yes—but it's also not a no, so I go on. "Why did you call my room last night? Were you looking for someone, or do you usually dial random numbers and talk to strange women?"

"Andi." He shakes his head, halting my words, but the way he says my name, the way he looks at me, it's like he is holding an invisible knife about to stab deeply into my chest.

"Just tell me."

He looks at my face, his eyes glazing over, sinking into a faraway memory. Trepidation eats away at me. I suck in a deep breath. It was good while it lasted, even if it was only a few good hours. I could cling to them. My mind is already creating all the worst-case scenarios it can, and I am drowning before he even opens his mouth.

"It was our room." His voice cracks a little as he speaks and spears my heart.

"Our?"

He clears his throat and brings his fingers to his eyes, squeezing them shut and pinching the bridge of his nose before drawing in a long breath and finding my eyes with his own. "We stayed here, just once. After we'd been together for six months. It was my birthday and she wanted to do something special for me." He swallows hard. "We had the most amazing night." He shakes his head, and I realise he is plagued by her shadow.

"So you keep calling the room?" The rest of my questions go unasked as he shrugs.

"How many times have you called? Did you get all those women to—"

"It doesn't matter, Andi." His hand squeezes mine.

"Because not a single one of those people cared enough to ask me what *I* wanted, how *I* was. But you did. It doesn't matter what I was looking for; some ghost of a past that was never really meant to be, because somehow, it led me to you."

I let out a long breath and sit back into my chair, my mind muddled and clear all at the same time.

"Would you like to come to my book launch later today?" Butterflies erupt in my stomach, and I feel suddenly sick. Why the hell did I just ask him to come? What if tonight is worse than yesterday?

"I would." He smiles at me, and it's too late to take it away. "Are you okay?" He reads my anxiety.

"I'm nervous."

"Don't be." He stands up and holds his hand out to me. "What should we do till then?"

⸻

Dean

Isi finishes her coffee, and she still looks wrecked. I wonder for a while at the kind of night she could have had with that stuck-up prick. He looked like a two-pump bandit, but for now, it doesn't matter. I have her here with me like I wanted last night. She is exactly what I was looking for, ticking all my boxes with her long blonde hair, curvy body and sweet smile. She screams innocence, and it's just the kind of girl that gets me all hot on the inside. Now that I finally have her, I'm not letting her go a second time. Maybe this experience hasn't been a waste of time after all. Two birds, one stone and all. Margot was a great consolation prize but Isi, she is the cherry on top that will have all my urges met.

I give her my best boyish smile, the one I have learned to perfect, and her face lights up. Girls tend to believe they want the bad guy, but really, they seek a guy like me that projects wholesome goodness. I've worked very hard at looking my best and being that good guy. Holding down a good job, driving a car that shows I've got money in the bank, looking after my body and appearance, not to mention my nobility—that shit is hard, but girls lap it up.

"Can I give you a lift somewhere?"

"Oh, no it's okay, I can grab an Uber."

"Why? I have a car right downstairs in the parking garage."

She yawns again, and I smile brighter. Between the night she's had and the drops I put in her drink, she won't last much longer.

"I don't want to be a bother."

"You won't be. I have nowhere to be, and you look... exhausted." I know she can read what I'm actually trying to say; that everyone in this breakfast buffet knows that she's been thoroughly fucked and is going home in last night's dress.

"I am pretty tired."

"Save your money."

"Are you sure? I don't live far from here."

"Of course."

"Okay." She's beaming at me.

"Great, then it's settled."

We get up, and she stumbles a little. I reach for her and take her hand. It's so fucking soft I want to cry. At least I know what I have to enjoy later.

I lead her to the elevator and press the button for the basement where my car is parked. My tools and knives sit patiently in the boot waiting, and my fingers itch to get to work. I feel like a starving man, and though last night's fuckfest helped sate some of the savage beast that has been screaming inside me, it's suddenly this morning I am fucking giddy about. And the best part? She is covered in someone else's DNA. I saw the card she had in her hand, a phone number and all. When they find her, they won't be looking for me.

I smile at her again as I lead her to my car. The hotel cameras would have caught us leaving together, but Frank—the security guy—will start his shift soon, and he gets paid enough to make sure the footage disappears when I do. That, or his missus will lose another finger. I smile. That was a fun night. Not for them of course. But god that woman can scream.

Isi sighs heavily as I help her slip into the front passenger side. She'll be asleep soon, and when she wakes up... god, I am so fucking happy.

"You look happy," she tells me as her eyelids grow heavier.

"I had a good night, and my day is shaping up to be pretty good too."

She smiles at me all innocent and beautiful. "Yeah, it is."

I get in the car, slip on my sunglasses and drive into the morning.

If you enjoyed this books, please consider leaving a review on Amazon and Goodreads.

ACKNOWLEDGMENTS

I would like to start by thanking you the reader, so much for reading! If you enjoyed the story, please leave a review and recommend the book to any friend you think would love this story. You will have my eternal love and gratitude.

A massive thank you to Tracey Caldwell, your input and encouragement has been amazing as always you inspire me in more ways than one.

Margot – thanks for the sprints the laughs and the encouragement – love you Ladyface.

To K - You always give me direction, elevate my writing and push me for more – you know – getting through all those practice drafts...You know what it all means to me, but I will never get why you drink the hot fruit juice when there is perfectly good coffee waiting for you... Thank you x.

ABOUT THE AUTHOR

Jane Wynters doesn't quite know how to answer the question of "where are you from?" She's moved from place to place like a snowflake on the wind always searching for a safe place to land. She loves meeting new people and exploring new places. She loves reading, writing and conjuring new worlds from her imagination. Coffee is at the top of her food pyramid and she is fluent in three languages, her favourite being sarcasm.

Want to know more about the author and keep in touch? Get snippets of upcoming books and have a bit of twisted fun?

Come join me in Wonderland...

ALSO BY J. A. WYNTERS

Standalones

Guarding Gabriel

The Beverage Wars

Mai Tais and Goodbyes

Fractured

Losing Liam

Parts of Me Series

Spare Parts, Book 1

Fixed Parts, Book 2

Broken Parts, Book 3

Coming Soon...

Torn Apart, Book 4

Picked Apart, Book 5

The Fractured Fairytale Series

Beast

Wolf

Hunter

Dreamer